PENGUIN BOOKS
FISH IN A DWINDLING LAKE

Ambai is the nom de plume of Dr C.S. Lakshmi, a historian and a creative writer in Tamil who writes about love, relationships, quests and journeys in the Tamil region and elsewhere. Her stories have been translated by Lakshmi Holmström in two volumes entitled *A Purple Sea* and *In a Forest, a Deer*. Ambai was awarded the Lifetime Literary Achievement Award of Tamil Literary Garden, University of Toronto, Canada, for the year 2008.

An independent researcher in Women's Studies for the last thirty-five years, Ambai is the author of several critical books and articles. She is currently the Director of SPARROW (Sound & Picture Archives for Research on Women). She lives in Mumbai with her film-maker husband Vishnu Mathur, in a small third-floor flat with a view of the sea, along with her fifteen-year-old foster daughter, Khintu, and her two little brothers, Krishna and Sonu.

~

Lakshmi Holmström is a writer and translator. She has translated short stories, novels and poetry by the major contemporary writers in Tamil. Her most recent books are *The Rapids of a Great River: The Penguin Book of Tamil Poetry* (2009), of which she is a co-editor, and *The Hour Past Midnight* (2009), a translation of a novel by Salma. In 2000 she received the Crossword Book Award for her translation of *Karukku* by Bama; in 2007 she shared the Hutch-Crossword Award for her translation of Ambai's short stories, *In a Forest, a Deer*; and in 2008 she received the Iyal Award of Tamil Literary Garden, Canada. During 2003–06, she was a Royal Literary Fund writing fellow at the University of East Anglia. She is one of the founding trustees of SALIDAA (South Asian Diaspora Literature and Arts Archive).

FISH
IN A
DWINDLING
LAKE

AMBAI

TRANSLATED BY LAKSHMI HOLMSTRÖM

PENGUIN BOOKS

PENGUIN BOOKS
Published by the Penguin Group
Penguin Books India Pvt. Ltd, 11 Community Centre, Panchsheel Park,
New Delhi 110 017, India
Penguin Group (USA) Inc., 375 Hudson Street, New York, New York 10014,
USA
Penguin Group (Canada), 90 Eglinton Avenue East, Suite 700, Toronto, Ontario,
M4P 2Y3, Canada (a division of Pearson Penguin Canada Inc.)
Penguin Books Ltd, 80 Strand, London WC2R 0RL, England
Penguin Ireland, 25 St Stephen's Green, Dublin 2, Ireland (a division of Penguin
Books Ltd)
Penguin Group (Australia), 250 Camberwell Road, Camberwell, Victoria 3124,
Australia (a division of Pearson Australia Group Pty Ltd)
Penguin Group (NZ), 67 Apollo Drive, Rosedale, Auckland 0632,
New Zealand (a division of Pearson New Zealand Ltd)
Penguin Group (South Africa) (Pty) Ltd, 24 Sturdee Avenue, Rosebank,
Johannesburg 2196, South Africa

Penguin Books Ltd, Registered Offices: 80 Strand, London WC2R 0RL,
England

First published by Penguin Books India 2012

Copyright © C.S. Lakshmi 2012
This translation copyright © Lakshmi Holmström 2012

Typeset in Palatino Linotype by InoSoft Systems, Noida

Printed at Anubha Printers, Noida

Contents

Contents

Author's Preface

There is no end to the stories storytellers tell. Whether or not someone asks, 'Tell me a story', stories continue to spring up in our minds. Some day or the other, we will attempt to pull out one of those stories, relish it, and give it to others, so that they may relish it too. These stories were born out of such attempts.

With the death of my friend Sundara Ramasamy, the publication of this collection will not be accompanied by the incidents which used to lighten my heart when my anthologies came out: my eager anticipation of his comments, my screams of delight if his words were appreciative, and my engaging him in a mock-fight, if he was disparaging—as indeed he was capable of being. I feel this loss greatly. I have not been to Nagercoil since he passed away. Now, my stories have gone there instead. I am happy that they are being brought out by the publication department of *Kalachuvadu*, established by him.

In Mumbai, gazing past the tall coconut palms at the sea which the huge apartment blocks have not yet hidden, amidst a babel of voices—the Hindi of my Rajasthani life partner Vishnu, the multilingual, loud chatter of Nepal-born Khintu, who has grown up in our house for twelve years, and her two brothers, the Gujarati of Kanchan who is our domestic help, and the Marathi voices which encircle us—amidst all this, I write in Tamil. In Tamil Nadu, people have often asked me, quite respectfully, 'How do you manage to write in Tamil?' Fortunately, no one has asked me, 'Why do you write in Tamil?' Even if they were to ask me—I live at a distance, incognito—their words cannot reach my ears; and even if they did, what does it matter? Do storytellers ever feel ashamed? Even if you drive them into the forest, they will go about telling their tales to the trees, the creepers and bushes, the flowers and birds and forest beasts, the rivers with their unknown sources. I am indeed such a storyteller. So long as there are stories in the mind, they will continue to take shape and form. They will reach someone's ears. It will be good enough even if they are heard only by the long-tailed green parrots that pay a visit every day to the big banyan tree next to our building.

Some of these stories have appeared in journals such as *Uyirmai, Uyirnizhal, Kalam, Kalachuvadu,* and *Panikudam.* Some have not yet been published.

My thanks to P.R. Subramanian, Secretary, Mozhi: all these years, whenever I have written a story, I have telephoned him without regard to time or place, pestering him to explain my many doubts, and he has always patiently answered my questions. My thanks also to Kannan: whenever I have telephoned concerning a detail to do with the publication, even if he was travelling or attending a meeting he has always responded with enthusiasm, never losing patience.

Ambai

Introduction

Ambai's short fiction spans more than thirty-five years and includes four anthologies: *Siragugal muriyum* (Wings may break) in 1976, *Viittin mulayiul oru samayalarai* (A kitchen in the corner of the house) in 1988, *Kaattil oru maan* (In a forest, a deer) in 2000, and *Vattrum eriyin miingal* (Fish in a dwindling lake) in 2007. Most of her earlier short stories have been translated into English, and published in the two collections *A Purple Sea* (1992) and *In a Forest, a Deer* (2006). Her most recent work is a set of short stories collected under the title, *Vattrum eriyin miingal*. We present all of them here, except for the initial story, 'A movement, a folder, some tears', which was included in the anthology, *In a Forest, a Deer*.

Some of Ambai's stories from her first two collections which make up *A Purple Sea* read like the fiction of ideas; of polemics, even. Such stories as 'Once again' and 'Vamanan' set out very clearly Ambai's criticism of the essentialism that polarizes 'male' and 'female' as different modes of functioning and being; a way of thinking that represents men and women as conditioned by their bodies, and which leads directly to the idealization of women as mothers. The weight of the argument might have overpowered the stories were it not for Ambai's invention of witty and new forms of fiction which allow the insertion of feminist discourse in a variety of ways. The most moving of the 1988 stories, however, involve a sensitive exploration of women's spaces, their words as well as their silences, their relationship with their bodies, their struggle against gender oppression and other constraints. 'A kitchen in the corner of the house' and 'Black Horse Square' remain as some of her finest stories.

The feminist themes continue, subtly and sensitively, in the collection *In a Forest, a Deer*. The title story, told beautifully as a fable, questions the notion of childless women as somehow barren, sorrowful, trapped within and by their bodies. 'Unpublished manuscript', 'Wrestling' and 'Forest'—all of which would stand among the finest stories that have appeared in Tamil in recent times—trace relationships which begin with a love affair and a marriage of choice. Each reflects the dilemmas, the politics and power struggles—and in particular, the professional jealousies—that can problematize marriages and families in modern India when traditional values still hold. In each case, the protagonist struggles to achieve autonomy.

The stories in *In a Forest*, however, have wider themes as well. An overriding concern is to do with understanding and defining one's identity in a changing world of exile and migration, both within and outside one's country; a world, moreover, where religious fundamentalisms have begun to prevail. 'A rose-coloured sari', 'Forest', and 'A movement, a folder, some tears' are all explorations of the struggle by women (and men too) to break free, not only of gender constraints, but also of the bondage of ideologies; to let go of identities one is forced into, one way or another; to allow for fluidity and change, but also to seek a grounded and unique self.

The current collection consists of eleven short stories translated from Tamil; it showcases Ambai's technical skills at her mature best. Her style can be elegant, witty and lyrical by turns. She has a sensitive feel for the landscapes of Tamil Nadu, but also a fine eye for the eccentric or unusual aspects of Mumbai. Some of her short stories work through ironic juxtaposition of incidents, or through repetition of images, as in poems. The longer stories, on the other hand, while still using the repeated symbol or motif, are intricately constructed, moving back and forth in time almost cinematically, interweaving different kinds of texts and narratives.

Seven of the stories are entitled, 'Payanam', Journey, numbered from 4 to 10; they complete a series begun in the previous collection, *In a Forest*, which includes, interspersed among others, the three earlier stories, 'Journey' 1, 2, and 3. The motif of the journey or quest is, in many ways, the linking image, threading through this entire collection; and, at the same time, the idea of the journey suggests a connection with her earlier work. Thus, the 'journey' or quest—both in actual and symbolic terms—points to the continuation and ongoing nature of certain of her themes, but also to a development, a journey further.

The journeys are of different sorts: sometimes by long-distance bus, or by autorickshaw, and in one case, by a hired taxi. But most often, they are by train. The railway station becomes a symbol of the teeming nature and energy of Mumbai in particular: a place where many strange meetings take place, many migrations. The suburban railway is also marked by some of the most tragic incidents of communal violence, in recent times. Journey 6 captures a vivid moment of that horror.

It is worth noting that all these shorter stories, simply entitled 'Journey' are narrated by an unnamed 'she' who is the traveller undertaking one journey, but who also witnesses another journey, hears another story. Some of the journeys end with the discovery of an unexpected or unconventional love affair, extraordinary tales of loyalty and integrity, as in Journeys 4 and 5. Others touch on the almost fantastic, absurd aspect of Mumbai, for example in Journeys 8 and 9. Here Ambai displays an amused, ironic tolerance towards the eccentricities and waywardness of human behaviour. Often they also indicate the discomforts, and hazards even, for women travelling alone.

The longer stories, central to the anthology, are not entitled 'Journey', but the motif of the journey is crucial to them all the same. They chart journeys of discovery: discovery of the whole and wholesome self, integrating the demands of the body as well as the mind. They chart, too, the loneliness and tragedy of those who fail to achieve such wholeness.

The first of these longer stories is the one entitled 'The calf who frolicked in the hall'. Once again, it is narrated by an unnamed 'she', from whose perspective the story unfolds. This is one of Ambai's most intricate stories. One narrative invokes scenes from the early seventies, a time of literary activity and hope, and the start of a new literary magazine, named, significantly, *Quest*. But this narrative is not told in chronological sequence. Instead, the ending of that hopeful time is remembered, even as its beginning is recalled; the end of the magazine also coinciding with the end of the love affair between the narrator and one of the magazine's editors, Kadir. Again, that story—itself interrupted sequentially—is intercut with the story of the narrator's meeting with Kadir in the United States, twenty-five years later. This story is marked by long car rides along the highways of the United States, during which Kadir and the narrator tell each other some of the incidents that have occurred in their lives during the long interval since they last met. During the last of these rides, she tries to explain to Kadir a little bit about the enigma of their friend Udayan's death, a story that she concludes after her return to India. 'The calf that frolicked' is most skilfully and poignantly constructed, the motif of a kiss woven through it, and standing for passion and its gentling, and also for death's leave-taking.

Ambai has spoken at length, in an interview with the Tamil journal, *Kalachuvadu* in 1997, of her literary development as a young woman, both in Delhi and Chennai, in the late sixties and early seventies; her encounters with some of the writers and critics of the time, such as Venkat Swaminathan and Indira Parthasarathy. Most of all, she says, it was through her intense friendships with the editors of the 'little magazine', *Pragnai* (Consciousness), during the time they spent together in Chennai, discussing, exploring, arguing, analysing, that she 'grew up' as a writer. Ambai draws on this experience in the story. The narrator of 'The calf' satirizes what she sees as the main characteristic of Tamil writing of the seventies, its focus on male angst and alienation, and its failure to understand the difficulties facing women as they fight hard within patriarchies 'to create (themselves) out of the evidence of their own being'. The failure of the journal mirrors, in a way, the failure of the love affair between the narrator and Kadir. Whereas she has already fought hard for her independence, and is free enough to choose whom she will love, honest enough to recognize and acknowledge sexual passion, he—for all his progressive views—is still bound to the family and its mores.

The intellectual restlessness, the disaffection and alienation with the world which characterized the seventies literati, is a continuing attribute of Udayan, most of all. In the end, his suicide, the narrator suggests, is his choice; his escape from attachment or responsibility. The reference to the *Tirumandiram* in his journal is an indication of his state of mind: '. . . without movement, without direction/ without cause or reason/ as if in delusion/ the body is cared for.' A similar restlessness and lack of commitment—even though he is married happily, with grown-up children—characterizes Kadir, too. The long car journeys symbolize his rootlessness. His words in the last letter to the narrator are almost as significant as the lines from *Tirumandiram* which end the story. He writes: 'You have your feet planted firmly in some place, somewhere. As for me, I feel as though beneath my feet there is nothing but air . . . I think one day I will die during a car journey, on an American highway . . . '

In the second of the 'key' stories, 'Kailasam', Ambai returns to a favourite theme of hers: her exploration of ways of 'seeing' and 'reading' the female body from a female perspective. The epiphanic moments in 'A kitchen in the corner of the house,' and 'Black Horse Square', both from *A Purple Sea*, and the title story of *In a Forest, a Deer* are all moments of sudden insight, recognition of a different notion of female beauty, a means of rare communication between women. Again, the theme of a growing awareness by a girl, a woman, of her own body and its needs, has never been far away from all Ambai's stories. It is also a theme that links 'A calf that frolicked in the hall' with the other two central long stories of this volume. 'Kailasam', however, is focused entirely on a woman's reading and understanding of her body, at different stages of her life, as it ages and changes: this is its main theme.

The story begins in a light-hearted vein, as the protagonist Kamalam recalls her college days, when she and her friends in a women's hostel were first beginning to be aware, not only of their own bodies, but the bodies of their male colleagues as well. They had gone through a playful phase, of bestowing daring nicknames with salacious sexual connotations on all the men that they knew. When, a rather serious older student, Sivagnanam, nicknamed Kailasam, suddenly proposes to Kamalam in passionate terms, she is shocked, and repulses him summarily. Kailasam, goes on to live as a lonely and reclusive academic in Coimbatore. Shortly after his retirement, he is found dead in the Sankey Lake of Bangalore. He leaves behind a notebook with only a few entries, spreading over two years, 1974 to 1975, when he first met Kamalam. The rest of the story consists of Kailasam's entries, which Kamalam reads, and her extended reflections which follow.

Following her reading of Kailasam's notebook, Kamalam recalls her own developing awareness, over the years, of love, desire and sexuality. She learnt only gradually, she reflects, through different relationships with men, to experience her body as if it were a 'natural landscape'. She learns to take control over her body, and to accept it 'with all its faults and merits, neither over-rating it nor undervaluing it'. She learns about the mutuality of passion. As an older woman, now, she tells Kailasam, in her final imagined conversation, 'When I consider my body as if it were a text, I see that it isn't a stable text. It changes. Its appearances and meanings keep changing.' Her final wish for Kailasam, now dead and cremated, is for his ashes to be scattered in a river, to enable some distant shore at least to be fruitful.

The story is remarkable for several reasons. Its lack of inhibition is one. Even for Ambai, this is new territory; nowhere else has she examined this theme of a woman's developing sexuality in such depth. The tone and language are finely judged. The *double entendres* embedded in the nicknames the girls choose are deliberately crude, yet oddly innocent; the girls know that they are, in a way, verbal experiments with sex. Kailasam's explosive notebook entries are explicit without being pornographic; if anything, they err on the lyrical. The trope of the body as a landscape, a changing landscape, is one of the most interesting aspects of the language that Ambai uses here. Kailasam describes himself as 'a rough piece of earth, full of stones, thorny'; in his imagination, Kamalam's body is associated with a river or a sea, she 'is also like a marshy land'. Inevitably we are reminded of the language of Sangam *akam* poems, where the sharply etched detail from the natural landscape of Tamil Nadu in the poem enables its erotic charge. The image of the 'red earth and pouring rain', in A.K. Ramanujan's beautiful translation of one of the best-known Sangam poems, for example, works precisely in this way. The erotic entries in Kailasam's notebook, though, are tragic: they are of desire unfulfilled. On the other hand, the 'truth of the body' as Ambai puts in her critical work, *The Face Behind the Mask*, is in Kamalam's long and honest reflection, which includes her description of the withering of the body, the subduing of passion, but not its loss; of change, acceptance of change.

The title story, 'Fish in a dwindling lake', is central to the collection, and a crucial one in Ambai's entire oeuvre, to date. In her earlier critical writings, starting with *The Face Behind the Mask'*, Ambai (writing as C.S. Lakshmi) has been critical, indeed scornful, of the 'mind/body split', or the opposition between 'love' and 'sex', in the writings of Tamil women. Here she returns to that debate, in more subtle and moving terms, through the stories of two women, Kumud and Bimla. Which is the more real, the experiential life, the life of the body, or some other life that aspires to something other, which seems to deny bodily pains and pleasure?

The two women, brought together in their college days because of their similar rural background, grow apart in the coming years. Kumud, a child widow, pursues an academic career, at which she is highly successful. Yet she has remained a widow and there are moments when she bitterly regrets her lack of a sexually and biologically fulfilled life, which she believes has been denied her. Bimla, on the other hand, never married. She lives a life of renunciation and social service, inspired by an unusual—and in some ways maverick—swamiji.

When the friends meet after several years, Kumud finds Bimla in pain, very slowly recovering from a long period of ill-health. She is still planning new schemes, though:

a school for the local children, a hospital, a rose garden. The confrontation between the two friends is crucial. Kumud insists that though Bimla has always denied it, it is the body, *udal*, alone, with all its pains, its hungers and thirst that is the truth. In her turn, Bimla declares she has never denied that. But, she wants to make that 'truth' more inclusive, much larger:

'The truth of each individual body is different. The body is indeed an anchorage. But each body casts anchor in a different sea. Everything external—trees and plants, creepers, forests, beasts—all of it is the body. Only the body. Without the body, there is nothing. Everything is through the body. You can stretch the boundaries and limits of the body continuously. It will accept everything, contain everything.'

The importance of understanding the body, of 'seeing' it truthfully without being 'trapped' by it, has been an underlying theme in Ambai's fiction for some time. But in this story she articulates it in these terms. Now Kumud, too, baffled and irritated initially by Bimla's words, has her epiphany later that evening:

'Kumud stood there until she was drenched to the skin. The rain water seeped through her, with the chill wind, she felt as if she had been scoured clean. The barbed-wire fence she held, the withered trees accepting the rain, the pond which lay there like a thirsty mouth opening, Chunari with her little skirt, the small boy who bought her bananas in that crowd-tossed bus-station, anticipating her hunger, the snow-covered mountain peaks he said you could see when the skies cleared—everything entered her body and came out again, spreading, spreading everywhere. Her body diminished into a dot, a single dot among several, all strung together.'

When asked about the senses in which she uses the word *udal*, body, Ambai has been adamant. In an email to this translator on 26 May 2010 she wrote: 'The only reality is the body, for everything comes with it. We exist because the body exists. When the body perishes nothing is left. Breath (life), self, mind, consciousness are all contained in the body. When there is no body, none of this is there either.' The passage above, makes equal sense then, in Ambai's terms, if we read 'everything entered her consciousness/ mind/self . . .' with the proviso that all these are contained in the body, the only vehicle of life. The body, as a vessel of consciousness, also becomes a 'tool' (as Ambai put it in another email) for mapping the external universe; a means of perceiving things seen in the external world as distinct, and distinctly present (the rain, the barbed-wire fence, the snow-covered mountain peaks, etc . . .), but 'strung together', all the same.

Reading Ambai's work as a whole, then, it becomes clear how far beyond her early feminist polemics she has come. She never loses sight of her aim to explore a woman's relationship to her body as truthfully as possible, but arrives at a far more complex notion of that 'body'. Her later fiction raises a number of philosophical questions, but wisely, she deals with large questions such as the nature of the self, and of being, through her fictional characters and their life experience, without authorial intervention. Modern fiction, after all, is the very genre for the exploration of these complex themes.

Lakshmi Holmström

References

Ambai. 1998. Interview with Kannan and Manushyaputtiran. *Kalachuvadu* 20, pp. 25-40.

Ambai. 1997. *A Purple Sea.* Translated by Lakshmi Holmström. 2nd edn. Madras: East-West Books.

Ambai. 2006. *In a Forest, a Deer.* Translated by Lakshmi Holmström. New Delhi: Oxford University Press.

Lakshmi, C.S. 1984. *The Face Behind the Mask: Women in Tamil Literature.* New Delhi: Vikas.

Ramanujan, A.K. 1985. *Poems of Love and War.* New Delhi: Oxford University Press.

Acknowledgements

I thank Ambai for her patience and readiness in answering all my questions. It is always a privilege and a pleasure to translate her work.

Thanks also to Kamini Mahadevan, consultant editor, Penguin Books India for her encouragement and to Mark Holmström for his support.

Part of the introduction is taken from a paper presented at a conference on 'Tamil Literature Today' at the University of Chicago in 2010 ('Mapping the body, mapping the world: Ambai, Sukirtharani, Kuttirevathi').

Journey 4

There was still some time before the bus would start. She had already demolished a paper packet of peanuts, following it with a ginger *muraba*, just to aid the digestion. Still no sign of the driver. Next to her, a pregnant woman, on a seat meant for three passengers. She looked as if she were five or six months gone. Wrists covered in bangles: red, yellow, green and dark blue. Around her neck, chains, *tali*, mango-patterned necklace, etc. The middle-aged woman beside her—possibly her mother—kept blotting the sweat off her forehead, shoulders and neck with a small towel. She touched the younger woman as gently as she would, a bird. 'How it's pouring off you! At least when the bus starts there will be a bit of a breeze,' she said, fanning the girl with the newspaper she held in her hand. The pregnant girl accepted all her mother's attentions with quiet pride. At the same time, she was mindful of the young man who stood outside, beneath the window. He, for his part, continued to hand her, one after the other, a tender coconut, gram sweets, *murukku*, bananas and so on.

'Come back soon. Don't stay on there,' he said, standing solidly there. Firmly moulded arms and legs. A body like a rock.

'I've told Bakkiyam-anni to send you your meals. Eat properly. And don't go about in the heat, ayya. It's not good for you,' she told him, again and again..

The same conversation might have been repeated ten times over, without change of tone. Yet it seemed to contain different meanings each time. The expressions on the speakers' faces kept changing too, showing in turn elation, fond reproof, playfulness, laughter, tenderness, yearning, and sadness at parting.

Now and then the mother intervened to say, 'Why don't you let Thambi go home? He shouldn't have to stand there in the sun.'

The driver jumped in and sat down. Noises preparatory to starting the journey ensued. All at once, the man standing beneath the window began to cry.

'Go and return safely. I'll be yearning for you,' he said, sobbing hugely, and crying aloud.

The girl was shaken. Greatly anxious, she said, 'Don't cry. I'll be back. I'll be back very soon.' He wept the more. Broken words came from him, 'The house, so lonely . . .'

The girl rose to her feet. 'Ayya, should I just stay here? Will you go on your own?' she asked piteously, wiping her tears.

'No, no. It's a wedding in your relative's house. You must go. But come back quickly,' he said.

The bus began to move slowly. The girl leaned forward and stretched out her hands to reach him. He touched her fingers, then laid his hands against his cheeks. 'Go safely, Kamalam,' he said, breaking down yet again.

The bus began to pick up speed. The words 'careful', 'heat' and 'food' mingled with the wind and were lost. As the bus left the station and turned into the main street, when they looked back, they could see him standing in exactly the same place; his whole self shaken, his shoulders rising and falling soundlessly. The girl must have caught sight of him.

'He's still crying,' she announced. 'He's like an innocent child. He won't even realize when he's hungry,' she said.

'Oh, really. It's not a year since you married. Did he stay hungry before that? He's his father's only son. After the woman of the house died, his father brought him up, didn't he? What are you talking about?' The mother snapped at her.

'You don't know anything, ayya. Within four months of arranging his son's marriage, my father-in-law went off on his countrywide pilgrimage. No, he'll be all alone at home. Only a wife knows what goes on inside a house.' The girl's eyes filled with tears.

'As if he's the most fantastic husband around town! I've borne four children, remember? Are you trying to teach me?'

'Let's say he is a fantastic man. He's certainly better than the bridegroom you wanted to tie me to—the one who demanded another half sovereign's worth of gold and a motor cycle before he would put a tali on me.'

'Why do you want to rake up that old story now? You just go to sleep,' the mother consoled her, laying the girl's head against her shoulder.

The girl laid her head on her mother's shoulder and went to sleep, her handloom sari of green with yellow checks

3

tucked conveniently at her waist, her stomach slightly raised, her bangles jingling each time she moved.

When the bus stopped at Nagercoil, several people had arrived to meet mother and daughter. A small girl in a rose-coloured *paavaadai*, who wore butterfly-shaped slides studded with brightly coloured stones in her hair, hugged the young woman, calling her 'Athe'. A young boy who looked as if he had just begun to wear long trousers came and stood next to her. Love, sympathy and contentment on all their faces.

~

When she had finished her work, her friend told her she must not leave Nagercoil without going to Kanyakumari. At Kanyakumari, waves like shoals of whales. Yet as they touched the feet they were as gentle as a kitten's tongue. The sun, smeared in liquid orange. When she turned her head to take in the full sweep of the sea, the girl came within her orbit. The pregnant girl on the bus. She was standing by the waves, at a little distance from her relatives. A round vessel with a lid in her hand. There was a tenderness in her expression as she gazed at the sea. Like a mother looking at her child. A softness played on her face, reminiscent of Balasaraswati when she mimed gazing at the Baby Krishna in his cradle, as she danced to the song *Jagadhodharana aadisathalu Yasoda*, 'Yasoda played with the saviour of the universe'. Was she looking at the sea, or at some illusory form? Even as she gazed at her, the young woman turned sharply towards her, returned her look for a second, and recognized her. She came forward, smiling.

'Watching the sea?'

'Yes; I've never seen it before. How the waves beat against the shore! I want to watch it forever.'

'Did the wedding go off well?'

'Mm. All of us are here together. We'll be leaving soon.'

'You'll go back home soon, won't you? Your husband was in tears, wasn't he, poor man!'

She smiled. 'Yes, he wept. He's got a heart as soft as cotton-wool, akka.' She stopped, then repeated, 'A heart as soft as cotton-wool.' She looked at the sea.

'My family looked for a different bridegroom for me. That man worked in a government office. He seemed all right. But when we were about to buy the wedding clothes, he cut in, "So you are going to spend two thousand rupees on her sari, but only eight hundred on my *vetti*? In that case I must have two vettis." People in our town laughed amongst themselves, "What's this! He's talking like a child!" But gradually the whole story changed. Before he would tie the tali, he claimed that the wedding jewellery was short by half a sovereign's worth, and demanded that it should be made good immediately, besides a promise of a motor bike within the month. It turned into quite a fracas. My sister held my brother-in-law's chin and pleaded, "Let me give her the chain I'm wearing round my neck." Something like a frenzy came over me, at that time, akka. I rose to my feet and rushed outside. I said, "I don't want this bridegroom. I will not marry him. If there is a man here who is willing to marry me as I am, then let him come forward." My voice was trembling. The base of my throat was hurting. Everyone was stunned. Their party said, "How brazen of her to say all this!" My family worried, "She's gone and thrown it all away by speaking out." Our townsfolk meanwhile, were wondering, "Who will marry her now, when she does this at such a tender age?" But then, his father came forward, bringing his son, his hand on his shoulder. His face was as innocent as milk. His body well set and sturdy. He was smiling slightly.

'The older man said, "This is my son. He is educated. He supervises my lands. There is no woman in our house; I have brought him up myself. He is willing to marry the girl. Ask her what she wishes." I stood there in shock. I looked at my father and nodded assent. I bowed to the departing bridegroom's people and said, "Stay and eat before you leave."

'And that's how this tali came to me, akka. He has such a good heart. A child-like heart.'

She stopped and looked at the sea. Then she continued, as if she were speaking to the sea. 'He dotes on children. All the children in our town come to him if they need anything. To fly kites, play ball, produce a play, to be taken to cricket matches. But a senior doctor has said that he of all people can't have children. It seems he wasn't looked after properly when he had mumps as a child, and became infertile as a result. He doesn't know this. He would die if he knew.'

Because of a short bus journey together, she was willing to take her entire life apart, and to share it. Responding to the glance on her slightly raised stomach, she said, 'This belongs to his family, absolutely.'

An image flashed through her mind of an older man on pilgrimage, dipping into and rising from many temple tanks.

'He's never seen the sea. If I catch the waves in this vessel, will they still be tossing when I show him, akka?'

She imagined a wave rising and falling within the small circular vessel. In the evening light, the pregnant girl who stood by the shore seemed one with the sea.

She could only touch her gently and say, 'No, you cannot capture the rise and fall of the sea's waves.'

Journey 5

As soon as she heard of the new highway which ran along the coast from Chennai to Pondicherry, she wanted to travel along it. Her Sri Lankan friend who now lived in Paris was visiting her at the time. She told her friend that she ought to see Pondicherry; it had once been a colony under the French. An illusion came over them both; as if Pondicherry were in some distant land, where they could take wings on arrival, and fly as they pleased. They began to make plans for the journey, and what they would do there.

The Sri Lankan friend was a lover of literature. She suggested they attend a literary meeting that was about to take place there. The seminar in the morning. Then sightseeing around the town. In the evening, the sea. Thereafter . . .

They began to plan for the late evening with excessive zeal. Pondicherry was a place once occupied by the French. There would definitely be bars there. The women there would most certainly be connoisseurs of wine. But would they also serve spiced gram, as they did in the bars in

Bangalore? When she raised this question, the Sri Lankan held a hand to her chest as if she had just had a heart attack, and berated her soundly in Sri Lankan Tamil. *Sundal*? Were they going all the way to Pondicherry only to eat sundal? When would she abandon her sundal fixation and turn her thoughts to fish, crab and fried blood? She managed to pacify her eventually, and drag her back to consider their late evening in Pondicherry. The Sri Lankan sighed deeply, like someone who had just come out of a state of possession, and controlled her anger. After that, their plans began to expand hugely.

They worked it all out in wonderful detail. They imagined how they would sit in a bar in the evening, drinking vodka and conversing late into the night about the tribulations they had encountered in their lives, their love affairs, all that was deeply engraved in their hearts—the music, the literature, the friends who had made life sweet. It was almost as if they were already in Pondicherry, even before the journey there.

The driver of the vehicle they had arranged to take them to Pondicherry was full of an eager desire to introduce her and the Sri Lankan friend to the culture of Tamil Nadu. He began to play cassettes of Tamil songs generously sprinkled with Hindi and English words, and interspersed with sighs, whimpers and whistles. This, at the very start of their journey. She and her friend had spent their school days in the company of films such as *Parasakti* and *Manohara*. They had sung the lullaby, *Kanne kanmaniye*, 'My dear one, my darling,' in melting tones to the babies in their families. They had immersed themselves in the voice of A.M. Raja, and his sorrowful songs such as *Sirpi sedukkaada porchilaye*, 'O golden

9

statue which no sculptor carved'. When she cut short the driver's enthusiasm, and asked him please to put on the unadulterated Tamil songs she carried in her handbag instead, the man's cordiality fizzled out entirely. A look of disinterest spread over his face, as if to say, 'You are the passengers, I am your driver, that's all.' Intermittently he looked at them through his driving mirror, as if they were Stone-Age women. He was unmoved by the joyful cries with which they greeted the songs. So they spent their journey talking about the seductive quality of the songs they were listening to, and the images they evoked, laughing and screaming with delight. When he dropped them at the lodgings they had booked in Pondicherry, the driver's face shone with the light of a sage who had renounced all things of this world.

The literary meeting had been convened in order to analyse the works of a famous writer who had died several years ago. Many spoke about the secrets of his art. Some said that although his writing was of a very high order, he was given to using obscenities frequently in his speech, and that such words could not be repeated in the presence of women. What a great loss to literary history, the Sri Lankan friend said, that those obscenities would now never find a place among the tape recordings of that day's speeches.

As they sat by the sea shore that evening, they recalled that during their sightseeing earlier, they had not set eyes on a single bar in the town. She remembered then, a friend who lived in the city, a professor, whom she had not seen for a long time. When she contacted him on her telephone, he agreed happily to spend the evening with them. As soon as he joined them, she asked him where there might be a bar where they could sit and have a drink together. He hesitated. 'It's a long time since I went to such places. Nowadays I have given up such bad habits . . .' he began. He saw the expression on their faces, and ended, 'I don't drink nowadays.' But, he added, he had no objection whatever to sitting with them while they did. He would have to enquire about a suitable place, though. He assured them that he would do just that and began his enquiry with an autorickshaw driver who stood at a street corner.

'Look here, appa, would you know of a bar where respectable women can go?' he asked in a low voice.

The autorickshaw driver looked at the respectable women in question, and prepared with alacrity to take them where they wished.

'Are you outsiders?' he asked, as soon as they climbed in.

'I belong here,' the professor told him.

'I know of a good bar, sir. All the women there are outsiders, sir.' He turned round and gave them a friendly grin.

He stopped in front of a hotel along a somewhat dark street. She went ahead to have a look, and was greeted very hospitably by the proprietor.

'Come in, amma. Are you from out of town?' he asked.

She nodded, and asked, 'Do you have a bar here?'

'Of course we do,' he affirmed.

'A place where we can sit and have a drink?'

'How can there not be? For how many hours, amma? One hour or two? We charge by the hour, amma. We'll have a room for you very shortly. Where's your client, amma? Have you left him in the auto? Is he also from out of town?'

She hurried out as fast as she could and said, 'Come, let's go. This isn't a bar. It's another sort of place altogether.'

'*Ayyayyo*,' lamented the professor, 'I'm not used to going to such places.'

'Are you suggesting that we come to places like this every day?'

A youth came past, glanced at the professor and said, 'Good evening, sir.'

'O, good evening, good evening. These are some people I know. I'm just on my way home,' he said, twitching awkwardly. He leapt into the auto by himself and called out, 'Get going, appa.'

After they found another auto and arrived at their lodgings, the Sri Lankan friend cursed the professor roundly, using all the obscenities she possessed in her vocabulary, since, unfortunately, the obscenities the learned writer used failed to be recorded.

They came outside again, having determined to have an early dinner, and leave the next morning, when they saw him. He was an older man who had sat quietly towards one side, at the meeting, he had smiled at them during the tea and lunch breaks, and exchanged a word or two. Now he greeted them.

'Are you going out to dinner?' he asked. Immediately they began to tell him about the shattering of their Pondicherry dreams.

'*Adada*. You should have asked me. Come, let's go to my place,' he said, hailing an auto, and climbing in with them.

When they reached his house, a woman of about sixty-five opened the door and greeted them with a smile. 'This is my friend, Gomati Ammal,' he said, making the introductions. 'They wanted a drink, but they don't know this town. They've been wandering about unsuccessfully.'

'Do sit down. Would you like some wine? My daughter has just brought some from Paris. Or would you prefer something else? There's vodka,' Gomati Ammal said.

When it was established that she would have wine and the Sri Lankan friend would drink vodka, Gomati Ammal went inside and brought two wine glasses and one tall glass, all of which she placed on a stool. She set down another small glass, saying, 'Today I've made some fried crab. There's a fish curry, there's rice. You must stay and eat here with me.'

The older man brought a platter of fried gram and other snacks. In the living room there were several photographs of young women with the same features as Gomati Ammal; in some, they held small children in their arms. There was also a garlanded photograph of an older gentleman.

Gomati Ammal opened the bottle of wine with ease, and poured it into the glasses. She measured out the vodka, added orange juice, stirred in some ice cubes and gave it to the Sri Lankan friend. She gave her one of the glasses of wine, and took the other one herself. She then held out the smaller glass of orange juice towards the older man.

They raised their glasses to a sweet and unusual evening together. The wine was comforting in her throat. She looked at Gomati Ammal and began, 'He told us that you are his friend?'

'O yes. He belongs to the same village as I. In fact, he was always in and out of our house. Our houses were on adjoining streets. We went to the same school. He was two years above me, though,' Gomati Ammal said. She looked at him and smiled fondly.

'It was because of her that I gave up cigarettes, alcohol and meat—all that. She, though, has changed. I can't do that, can I?' The older man smiled.

'Yes, speak in riddles. How can they hope to understand?'

He pulled his chair forward just a little, sat back comfortably, and began to speak. 'Ours was only a small village. Near Tirunelveli. There was a lot of toing and froing between our two houses. Four or five of us always walked to school together. I don't know exactly when, but we fell in love. Once she saw me standing outside a small stall, and thought I must surely have been smoking with the other boys there; she wouldn't speak to me for three days after that. She wouldn't believe me when I denied it. I promised then, I would never smoke cigarettes. I went further than that and promised I would never drink or eat meat either. The fervour of a nineteen-year-old! To this day I have never gone back on my word.'

She said, 'We loved each other. But we couldn't be together. We belonged to different castes. Nor did they— his people—have what was considered sufficient means. My family was actually paying for his education. When they began to look for a bridegroom for me, I went to him and pleaded that we should run away together. He said, "Neither of us is old enough. Where should we go, and how should we live?" We wept. How we wept. I got married. He too married a girl from our very village; a girl who was in the same class as I, who studied with me. We met sometimes, on special occasions. We'd exchange words.'

Once more, she filled the wine glasses. She poured another vodka and orange.

'Three years ago my husband passed away. All my children now live abroad. He and the lady of his house came on a condolence visit. A month later I wrote to him, "I have lived all these years in accordance with your wish. Now at least let me be with you?" He came to me then. He comes twice a month. He is never asked at home, why and where he is going. Neither does she say anything when she sees me. After all she is a woman who studied with me, isn't she? Isn't she my friend?' Gomati Ammal's eyes filled a little.

'We came together, didn't we, at last? Why do you get upset?' the older man said, going up to her, and patting her on the shoulder. Gomati Ammal turned her head and laid her cheek on his hand, as it lay there.

'Shall we eat?' he asked.

'It's a good thing these two came; now I'll have company to share the fish,' Gomati Ammal said.

'What can I do? I gave my word, didn't I?' he laughed.

It was a feast: crab, fish and a curry of field beans; side dishes of fried okra, *appalam* and *vadagam*; and a vermicelli *payasam* hastily put together by Gomati Ammal.

The older man accompanied them back to their lodgings.

When they put out the lights and prepared to sleep, both of them carried in the topmost layer of their conscious minds, an image of a wrinkled cheek laid against a hand whose raised veins spoke of old age. They didn't play any music on their return journey. There was a song though, in their heads. In Jikki's thin and high-pitched voice.

The calf that frolicked in the hall

It felt cold to the touch. Like a wet kiss.

It wasn't that difficult to contact Kadir, who lived in the United States. He had written her a long letter in the past year, soon after Udayan's untimely death. He wrote that with Udayan's death, something within him died too.

A kind of distaste threaded through everything Udayan did. She used to tease him, saying that of the *navarasas*, he was the hero of the *bibhatsa rasa*, the disgust mode. One of his younger brothers had committed suicide, for no apparent reason. He had not been in contact with Udayan for several years. This brother lived in a narrow lane, in a single room occupied by four other men. There wasn't even a rope in the house for him to hang himself with. Nor was the ceiling of any height. Udayan's younger brother, on the other hand, was six foot two and a half inches tall; he strangled himself with great difficulty, using his own *veshti*. Kadir recalled, in his letter to her, Udayan writing to him about this incident. 'They sent me to bring home the body of a brother who had completely distanced himself from the family. Just as I was about to set off, my younger sister said to me, "He came to me out of the blue last month, and borrowed some money. He said it was for a gas stove. If the stove is in his room, please bring it away." I brought away my brother's body, and I didn't forget to bring the gas stove too. I trust that day was a joyous one for my sister.' So Udayan wrote.

Kadir said, in his letter to her, that Udayan was a man who had experienced an extreme alienation. Alienation perhaps was a phase in most people's lives. But for Udayan it was his entire life.

When she telephoned Kadir, it was that letter she remembered. A handwritten one. When she rang the telephone number he had given, Kadir himself picked up the phone. The very first sentence which came from her lips was about Udayan. She couldn't believe a whole year had gone by. 'I keep remembering him all the time, Kadir,' she said. 'I too,' he agreed. He said, in English, 'He had in his hand a very long thread which held me to the years we spent together. His death snapped that. I was tugged back forcibly, and fell upon those years.'

There was a silence after that. In the United States, silences are not allowed during a telephone call. But in order to speak after twenty-five years, silence was indeed necessary, after that initial exchange. Memory can move very swiftly. Words do not possess the same swiftness.

A senior official in a bank cannot allow time to freeze, however. 'And then? And then?' he pressed her.

And then they decided on a time to meet, and a place.

~

The early nineteen seventies. A time when some relationships came to an end suddenly. One relationship had lasted for six years. He was a married man. She fell easily into the web of stories he wove: his wife was an invalid; his intellectual thirst tormented him; his loneliness was his sorrow. It took all of six years to tear that web apart. And it was a small mouse that tore it. A mouse that cleverly brought her out—she who was caught in a spell and unaware of the web. She called him mouse, a man with a slight frame and a long face. 'If I'm a mouse, then you are a cat. A cat that holds me in its mouth,' he would say. She could not swallow the mouse. He would not let her swallow him. When she opened her mouth one day, he leapt away to his hole.

They were relationships that did her no damage. During the six-year relationship, her musical wings began to spread. That was when she was allured by Begum Akhtar's rendering of ghazals. Bhimsen Joshi, who could take a single line and create a whole world, found a permanent place in her house. Vaisnavite and Saivite bhaktas sat cross-legged comfortably, in her heart. The two-year relationship was different. It was a relationship closely involved with the world of Jazz, the Beatles, Joan Baez, and Bob Dylan; a relationship which introduced her to ganja. It reached a high point one night at about two o'clock, when she was somewhat stoned on ganja, conscious of Louis Armstrong's trumpet music rising like white smoke pervading everything.

One year she came to Chennai from Jamshedpur, for a training session. She was staying with a friend, before moving into the Working Women's Hostel on Poonamallee High Road. She had just arrived that morning. She met Udayan that very evening. When the bell rang, it was she who opened the door. He stood there with a big snake gourd dangling from his hands. He lifted it high, shook it from right to left and announced loudly in English, 'Today it's going to be a linga-puja meal in this house.' Her friend and his wife laughed and told her not to pay him any attention.

He invited her to eat at his room in T. Nagar the next day.

His was a small, tile-roofed room at the back of a large house. Books everywhere. He was not in any regular employment. Sometimes he worked; sometimes he didn't. The feast consisted of *sambar*, *poriyal* and *appalam*; that was all. As soon as they had finished, he told her, 'My friends and I have begun a new journal. I need to go and meet them.'

'Shall I come with you?'

He looked at her, as if he were taking in her sleeveless *choli* for the first time. 'We'll see. The elders in that family are a bit old-fashioned. I'm not sure whether they will let you in their house. What are my friends going to say, besides? Let's see.'

He left her standing outside the compound wall and went in. That was Kadir's house.

Kadir came out at once and invited her in. He berated Udayan.

The room in the front verandah was Kadir's. Cover designs for the journal were scattered all over his desk. It was a struggle to make out its name, *Thedal* (Quest). The letters making up the name wandered all over the page.

'What do you make of them,' asked Kadir.

'They look as if they're staggering about, drunk to the gills,' she said.

'Where have you brought her from?' Kadir asked Udayan. Laughter then.

~

In Kanchipuram, that night, they sat up for a long time, in the front *thinnai* of Amudan's house. Arangannal had left for his home. The lights had been put out in all the houses around. They could hear, only intermittently, small noises from different houses, and the occasional sound of a passing vehicle.

It was a while since *Thedal* had ceased to appear. They shared a feeling of inexplicable helplessness: a sense of closure and lack of closure, of structure and lack of structure, of order and utter disorder. Inexplicable emotions that fell apart, however much they tried to string them into words. Each of them was silent.

~

Kadir came to the house where she was staying, in order to pick her up. His face seemed to have hardened, a little. His eyes had lost their light. She searched for the compassion of poetry she once found there.

'Why do you look like that?'

'I'm looking to see if you have changed.'

'And have I?'

'That's how it strikes me.'

'Life here is a rat race. You cannot manage if you don't change. But don't worry; it's only a superficial change.'

'Where are we going for dinner?'

'Only to my house.'

'I hope that hasn't caused a lot of work.'

21

'What work? It's already prepared; I only have to reheat it in the oven and serve it.'

'No cooking?'

'Only during the weekend. There's no time during the week.'

'Was Shirley working today?'

'Shirley is not at home. She's gone to California on office work.'

'Children?'

'How will they not be at home? They are eager to meet their father's old girl friend.' Then he laughed.

'Why do you laugh?'

'You called them children, that's why. The boy is twenty. He's studying at Syracuse; he's here just for this week. The girl is eighteen; she's going to college right here.'

'Do they speak Tamil?'

'How will they speak Tamil? I can't talk Tamil to Shirley; only English, American English.'

'Then with whom do you speak Tamil?'

'It comes to me in my dreams. I wrote a few poems suddenly, last year.'

'Poems? You?'

She laughed.

He laughed with her.

∼

At first they subjected every word and action of hers to an intense critical scrutiny, as if under a microscope. There was Udayan's sarcasm on the one hand, Kadir's analysis on the other. There were two others. They were from Kanchipuram, and were punch-drunk on Marxist-Leninist ideology. These two were the theoretical supports for *Thedal*. They had set aside their real names and given themselves the pseudonyms Arangannal and Amudan. Their love of books bound these four together. Even in the densely occupied Ranganathan Street, it seemed they were in a remote island of their own as they read and discussed Camus, Sartre and Pablo Neruda. There were debates on T. Janakiraman, Indira Parthasarathy, Mauni and Asokamitran. They described themselves as travellers and tourists of literature. They declared they were not devotees who would undertake literary pilgrimages to Madurai, Tiruvananthapuram Tirunelveli, Nagercoil and Delhi. They were not prepared to go to the Literary Temples of Chennai, and prostrate before the icons there; they were only prepared to meet these deities when they circulated in the outside world. Only Coimbatore Kumarasamy, who shared with them all his experiences and thoughts, and supported them entirely, received their whole-hearted respect. Several issues of *Thedal* saw the light of day only after his forceful touch.

It was with him alone they were prepared to discuss, fight, and make peace. Kadir used to say, laughing, that you could enjoy a profound friendship with Kumarasamy, only if you stopped talking to him.

Intent on analysing her, they took apart, piece by piece, her dress, her words, her attitude, her ideas. She couldn't bear it. Once, when she went to Bangalore for another course in her training, she wrote a letter to them. 'You look at me as if I belong to some strange species. It really troubles me. I could speak, read, debate with you. But it can happen only if I'm one of you. Otherwise I will always be an outsider. Just a spectator.'

The letter brought a result. On the day she returned from

Bangalore, Kadir and Udayan were at the station. Flowers held in their hands. Smiling faces. They accompanied her all the way to Poonamallee. They waited while she had a bath, and then took her to a restaurant for breakfast.

'What's so special, dear friends?' she asked.

'No more cold war. Hereafter it's all cordiality,' said Kadir.

The good relations continued on every occasion she came to Chennai thereafter.

~

In the darkness of the thinnai they were all shadowed outlines. 'In the nineteen seventies, only an alienated middle-class young man stands as the symbol of Tamil youth,' she began. He was present in every story or poem which appeared in *Thedal*. A young man who was unemployed, scorned by his own family, who returned home late in the evening to eat the cold buttermilk-rice and lime pickle left for him in the corner of the kitchen; who lived with the sorrow of Being, and other such sorrows. Or else he was a young man trapped in a permanent job which his heart rejected and which gradually sapped his life; caught up in the aridity of daily life. He ate. He rushed to work. On Sundays he soaped his clothes and washed them. He even got married. Then he published a book and proclaimed his life of detachment with the words, 'This recently married man likes saffron, the colour of renunciation.' He was a young man who could neither break free of his family, nor live with them. The umbilical cord was still around his neck. Besides all this, he possessed a craze for literature. More, a craze for poetry.

~

It didn't seem likely that she would meet Kadir again, after that dinner. The conversation, somehow, didn't get anywhere. It went in many directions—literature, politics, culture—appeared to delve further, but fizzled out eventually. Before the marks were made, they were erased. His son and daughter conducted themselves very politely. Nothing could be faulted in the food, hospitality or conversation.

All the same. Something was discordant. The ascending and descending scales were all in perfect order, only the tune would not take shape. Besides, there was the cold.

After she had said her goodbyes, there was some kind of superficial conversation between them as he drove her home. Suddenly, after she had climbed out of the car, he came up behind her and wrapped a thick shawl around her. When she looked at him in surprise, he wore a smile such as she had not seen throughout the evening. Just as she crept into the comfort of her blanket that night, the telephone at her bedside rang. When she picked it up, wondering who would telephone her at that time of night, Kadir's voice sounded.

'Have you gone to bed?'

'Yes, just now.'

'You weren't happy with this evening's programme, were you?'

She was silent.

'Hey, it's a huge gap, twenty-five years.'

Her throat choked as she said, 'Yes.'

'You are able to melt instantly, like snow. That's your strength. It's all easy for you. For me, it takes a while. I have to wander though many different spaces, before I can even begin to meet you. Don't you know that? Sleep well.'

'You too.'

'I have some work I must finish. I can only go to bed after that. If you can't sleep, you must call me at any time. All right? I'm here. I'm not about to go anywhere.'

She put out the light and slept instantly and very soundly.

~

Every time she came to Chennai, as soon as her work was done, she would set off directly to the bank where they were employed. All the way back on the electric train from Beach station to Mambalam, they'd talk and laugh and joke noisily. When they reached Kadir's house, Udayan would be waiting there. Arangannal and Amudan would go to their own room and join them later. Theirs was a small thatched room built on the terrace of a house. Arangannal described such rooms as urban huts.

The first thing they did when they reached Kadir's house was to look at the post. Kadir's mother worked in a firm, and she usually arrived home a little before they did. Just as soon as Kadir changed into his veshti, her invitation would come from within, 'Here, come and take your tea.' Kadir would go in and return with the tea.

By the time Kadir's father came home, Arangannal and Amudan would have joined them. They'd make off to the terrace then. They worked furiously inside the thatched area. Udayan's blunt criticisms cut in now and then. Once, she declared that a poem Arangannal had translated contrived to upturn language itself, and started to read it out at the top of her voice. He tried to snatch it out of her hands, she ran away, while the rest rocked with laughter. In Kadir's mother's words, 'The whole of Mambalam was shocked to see such misbehaviour.'

It seemed that many years ago, Mambalam had been utterly shaken by Bhuvana of the corner house, who married for love. Kadir's mother gave them several instances to prove that Mambalam had been brought to the same state of shock now. When these words reached Kadir's father's ears, they came coloured by his mother's code of conduct. The older man, for his part, had no doubt at all that literature, music, painting and dance were all strongly linked to impropriety. Now, Kadir's father was not in the least concerned about her propriety, or lack of it. But the argument, 'The boy will be ruined' struck him forcibly. He told Kadir to behave in a less obtrusive manner. A long lecture followed, Kadir reported.

For some days following this, they met in Arangannal's room. Or else at Udayan's. Once the pillars of propriety belonging to the houses along Kadir's street, so shaken by witnessing their horseplay, were firmly in place again, they returned to Kadir's room.

~

The conversation continued into the night, as all other sounds died away.

So are women not bothered by questions about Being and Nothingness, Udayan and Kadir asked her.

Of course a woman reads Camus too. She reads Sartre. She also reads the *Tirumandiram*, Akka Mahadevi and the Sufi poets. But when the entire family is engaged in creating the head of the household, a man, she has to find the nooks and crannies where she can create herself

27

out of the evidence of her own being. It is because she continually asks herself philosophical questions concerning Being that she is able to redeem herself and come outside from the grave-pit of daily living. She lives in a world full of symbols. 'Why are you at the window?' is the question underlying her life. The window is the symbol of the world outside. Her freedom lies outside the window. Both the running stream and the stagnant well are her symbols, too. Symbols of death. Words such as 'I'll fall into the river or well and die' are the sounds of her language-world. She is always denounced, finally, as a prostitute.

'Fine. All this is mere breast-beating. Are you saying that women are sacrificial lambs, then? I can hear songs like "If you are born a woman, this world must always be sorrowful" playing away in the background,' Udayan said.

She denied it. A woman is aware of both the heaviness and the lightness of Being, she said. Sometimes, Non-being is itself her Being, she said. Sometimes she is when she is not. At other times, even when she is, she isn't.

~

The shawl that Kadir gave her was snug and warm against the chill American winter. The telephone sounded each evening. Kadir spoke to her. Gradually his voice grew warmer, gaining in warmth like a hearth being lit. When she remarked on it, he said nothing is ever lost forever.

It seemed as if her American trip was one long car journey. She made several trips with Kadir. Sometimes Shirley came too.

Sometimes they talked about some of the incidents that had happened during the twenty-five-year interval. Once when they were travelling along a seemingly endless highway, he asked her about one such incident. 'Amma wrote once. She said you visited her after Naomi was born; when she was about a year old. She said you had brought a silk *paavaadai* for the child.'

'True. I'd gone to Chennai on some work. Udayan gave me the news. I went to Nalli, bought the silk skirt-material and took it to your mother. She returned it saying you wouldn't dress the child in silk clothes.'

'She was right. We didn't put her in silk clothes.'

'I came outside with the silk. It was terribly hot. Your mother went back inside. Your remember the mango tree in front of your house? It had been chopped down. Only the base of the tree was left standing. I went and sat on it. You know how, when the sun is very bright, there is a sudden dazzling white that strikes across the eyes? I felt just that. Nearby they had erected a pump-set with a tap. I pumped up some water and washed my face. I drank some water, drenching my clothes. It felt suddenly as if in all of that great city of Chennai, there wasn't a single door I could knock on, Kadir. Udayan was somewhere in Tambaram. Amudan and Arangannal had lost touch with me entirely. I had continued to read everything that was published, but there was no way I could knock on the door of a writer and say, "I came to discuss literature with you." Everything, everything lay within limits and bounds. Except for myself.'

'And then?'

'I walked out of your compound, found a small stall, and drank a bottle of soda. I looked at the newspaper hanging there and found out what pictures were running at which air-conditioned theatre. I went to a comfortable air-conditioned theatre and bought a balcony seat. I fell asleep even before the titles finished appearing.'

She laughed.

'What did you do with the silk material?'

'You won't believe me if I tell you.'

'Go on. Tell me.'

'When the picture finished, I walked all the way back to the hotel where I was staying. There was a wayside shrine along the way. Some Amman shrine, Bhadrakali or Esakki. All stone and *kumkumam*. I draped the silk over the idol.'

'What colour was the silk?'

'Dark blue, patterned with stars.'

〜

A warmth and closeness sprung up between Kadir and herself, very quickly and naturally. On one occasion, as she arrived in Chennai, she was overcome with tiredness. She just could not go to the bank, as usual, to meet all of them. Neither could she bring herself to go to her hostel.

She decided to go directly to Kadir's verandah room, which was also the *Thedal* office. Udayan was there already, correcting proofs. As soon as she got there, she spread out a mat and lay down.

'Hey, what's happened?' he asked her.

'Udayan, please go and buy me two cups of hot tea and a Baralgan.'

'Why, what's wrong with you?'

'Nothing. Stomach ache. It's what happens every month.'

Udayan took the flask and ran.

She drank the tea, took the pill and lay curled up.

By the time Kadir and the rest arrived, her stomach churned with pain compounded by the tea. She went to the toilet adjoining the room, and threw up. After that, she began to feel a little more settled.

Later, when she had washed her face, they set off to the printing press. Kadir didn't take his eyes off her while she sat there.

That evening, when they had accompanied her to the hostel he asked, 'Does it ache a lot?'

'No. Not so much now,' she told him.

'Will you come tomorrow?'

'Yes, I'll come.'

'You know something? You know how I've got used to your coming to meet us in the evenings—when you weren't there today, I had a sudden dread. Then when I came home, you were lying there, all curled up. I was really frightened then.'

She held her hand out to him. 'Hold my hand, please.'

He hesitated a second, then took her hand in his. Slowly he tightened his grasp.

~

Stars lay in clusters against the Kanchipuram sky. As for the sky, it was that dark blue which Bharati's songs mention. After their initial conversation, they were all silent for a while. Then Udayan began again.

'It's true, nothing is clear. You can't hold on to anything. Even during the Independence struggle there were journals which held firm beliefs. They had forceful names, *Ezhuthu*, Writing; *Manikkodi*, Banner. Now, even the names of the journals show a lack of goals: *Vanampadi, Vaigai, Yatra, Kaatru, Padigal, Chuvadu* and so on . . .'

'Don't generalize,' said Kadir. 'There is still *Visvarupam*. Also *Kollipaavai. Darsanam. Gnanaratham.*'

'But are any of those names forceful, though? *Visvarupam*, Cosmic form; *Darsanam,* Vision; *Gnanaratham,* Chariot of wisdom . . . And what about us? *Thedal*! Quest! What quest?'

'Great, Udayan, you've started on your *ninda sthuthi*, have you, berating the deity on his failings?'

'Udayan's sarcasm, Thanjavur style,' she put in.

'That's right. I'll be sarcastic, you be abrasive.'

'This is good,' remarked Amudan. 'Sarcasm and abrasiveness. You could describe the clash between critics and writers in those terms.'

For the first time that evening, there was a sense of the ice melting.

∼

During another car journey, he asked about her family.

'Didn't Udayan give you any news about them?'

'He might have done. I can't remember.'

'After we all went our different ways, I didn't return to Chennai very often. I had my work in Jamshedpur. Within two years, my father died. Do you remember my younger brother, Mukund? Just as soon as he got himself a job, he insisted he would only marry a certain girl who had been in college with him. And immediately, at that. She was a fine girl, too. One day the two of them were going somewhere on their scooter, when a truck crashed into them. She died there and then, on the spot. Mukund suffered a severe blow to his spine. He is completely paralysed from his waist down. Now he can only go about in his wheelchair. My younger sister Gita is here, in the US. You saw her yesterday, didn't you? She spoke to you, didn't she?'

'Was that Gita? I didn't recognize her at all.'

'It's ages since you saw her. As soon as I said I was coming to this conference, she insisted stubbornly I should stay with her.'

'Didn't your mother come with you?'

'Amma isn't alive now.'

'Is it because of Mukund you've stayed single?'

'That's one reason. But it's not the only one. I now run the company that Appa started. We have a big house in Jamshedpur. I can't abandon all that. I have a network of good friends. It isn't as if being single leaves me wanting in any way. Gita's second daughter lives with me and goes to school in Jamshedpur.'

'But isn't love necessary too, in one's life?'

'How can it not be? But it doesn't last forever, it's something that comes and goes. Sometimes it's a delight when it happens. Sometimes it's a delight when it leaves. If it's there, it's a sadness at times. At times, if it isn't there, it's a sadness too. Don't imagine I haven't been sad, Kadir. Sometimes I am deeply, deeply sad. But even that's a comfort, too. Call it a kind of privilege.'

'Do you recall what Udayan used to say? He'd ask, "What's an unfulfilled love? What exactly has to be fulfilled?"'

'True. Once, when a friend of his married the girl he loved, he remarked, "Poor man, his love hasn't been fulfilled."'

'He had a way of plunging into seriousness, even when he was joking. Once we were on a bus together. Suddenly he turned to me and said, "If there weren't love, nobody would have talked about death."'

33

'In the end, he left us without telling us what he thought about death.'

'I can't understand why he made that decision.'

They sank into their own thoughts after that. The car moved on steadily.

~

One evening there was a huge, jostling crowd near the T. Nagar bus station. All of them were there, part of the crowd. The occasion was the unveiling of a statue of Periyar. The statue was still covered in its wraps. Next to it a high stage had been erected. In a little while, Ki. Viramani arrived. The crowds broke into cheers when the wraps were removed. In his speech, Viramani enunciated the Gayatri Mantra, giving each word a special emphasis. This was how brahmins say it, he told the crowd; Periyar was a man who opposed brahmins, he trumpeted. The speech was punctuated by clapping, whistling and frequent cries of, 'Well said'.

She had never heard Periyar speak. She knew of him only through the books she had read. Nor had she ever heard a speech such as this. She felt as if she were participating in a historic event. She too clapped her hands enthusiastically. She screamed with the rest of them. They were standing very near the stage. During a magical moment when she was shouting gleefully, she had the sudden illusion that the Periyar statue came alive and looked steadily at her. She leaned her head on Kadir's shoulder.

After the crowds had dispersed, it seemed to them they had been witnesses of history in the making. They walked along, all of them hand in hand. Because it was very late by then, they all lay down to sleep on the terrace floor.

Nobody else was at home that day, in Kadir's house. They talked for a long time, gazing at the mango tree's branches high above them, and the moon, and the night sky. About the Self- Respect Movement and the stagnancy of its current policy. They discussed the unveiling of the Periyar statue, debating whether it was a symbol of rationality, or an icon of someone newly deified.

Long after she had fallen asleep, sometime later that night, she felt Kadir's hand on her. That first kiss, soaking wet, went on for a long time. They lay there for a long time, seizing at each other's lips. His lips, cold at first gradually began to burn. 'Hamma,' he moaned from time to time.

~

When they finally finished talking and went inside, a tiny calf stood in the *kuudam*, the central hall of the house. The cow had calved that evening, even as they arrived in Kanchipuram. It stood there now, its legs still trembling. With its large wet eyes, the calf stood there like a small white fawn.

When she touched it, it gave a shudder. After they had finished dinner and were setting off to the thinnai, Amudan's mother had said, 'I've left the calf in the hall. It might gambol about in the night. You'd better warn the girl. I don't want her to be scared.' Amudan hugged it, and stroked it for awhile. From its stall in the back yard, the mother cow called for its young, 'Mma.' 'She will keep calling like that. But if we let her have the calf, she'll pretty nearly lick off its skin.' The calf nuzzled against him.

~

Kadir had to go to Syracuse on some business of his. He thought he should look up his son at the same time. She too had some relatives in Syracuse whom she needed to visit. They decided to go there by car. The arrangement was that after the Syracuse visit, she would go on to New York, and return home from there.

It was their farewell trip. Kadir didn't say much. After a little while, when the car had begun to run at a steady pace, she began.

'Kadir, I need to tell you something.'

'Go on, tell me.'

'Udayan and I were living together for ten years. It was after that, he died.'

He turned his head sharply, and looked at her.

'For some reason, he didn't want me to tell you. It all happened unintentionally. He was working at one thing or another, desultorily. He began many things. Never finished them. Once he told me, "If only I could find an evening job, it would suit me down to the ground. Then I could read all day, and work in the evenings." I found him such a job in my own company. I even arranged accommodation for him. A couple of months later he said, "The night shift doesn't suit me at all, I can't watch the stars." Again I found him a daytime job. In time, he was bored with that as well. He grew very close to Mukund, meanwhile. He would come and talk to him for a long time, every evening. He stayed on and ate with us. We used to look forward to his arrival, every evening, Mukund and I. One day I went up to his room and invited him myself, to move in with us. He came without standing on any ceremony. He moved in as naturally as if we had been living together for many, many years.'

'Did Arangannal and Amudan know about this?'

'I think they must have known. Udayan continued to go to Chennai from time to time. He might have told them. But they had broken off any contact with me, so I didn't know. He only hesitated to tell you.'

Kadir was silent. When they had gone a little further, he stopped the car at a petrol pump, and went in to buy two freezing-cold ice-cream cones. They began to eat them, as they sat in the car. He finished his quickly and started the car again.

Still eating her ice-cream, she turned and looked at him. His hair was cropped close to his head. It was beginning to go grey at the back. His neck appeared very long. She stroked the back of his neck, very gently.

~

Once when she was returning from Chennai to Jamshedpur, Kadir and Udayan came away with her. The three of them travelled around many cities together. Finally, they returned to Chennai together. Kadir and she were at a stage when their relationship was at its most intense. The stage when you want to be inseparable at all times. His parents were deeply upset by this. A tense atmosphere filled the house. Arguments went on every day. Udayan and the others did their best to protect the two from becoming too frustrated. All the same, she was hurt by his parents' stubborn opposition towards her. At the same time she was tormented to see how pained he was by his parents' taunting. She wished that they could return to the carefree days of old when they selected poems for *Thedal*; when they sat together on the steps of the printing press in Mylapore, waiting for the proofs; when they woke up at dawn and hurried out to watch the sunrise; when they travelled on the electric train in the evenings; when they went to the same picture seven or eight times in order to critique it properly; when they attended literary conventions as a group.

On that occasion, when she was returning to Jamshedpur, Kadir looked miserable. 'Do you really have to go?' he asked her. As the train began to move, he held her hand and pleaded, 'Come back soon.' She wrote him a long letter soon after she reached home. That letter was to be the cause of a great disaster.

The letter which came from him, made no mention of the one she had already sent. Soon after that, when her father returned home from his office one day, he asked her, 'Did you send Kadir a letter recently, amma?'

'Yes, Appa. Why?'

'His parents seem to have intercepted and read it. It seems they have a relative here, in Jamshedpur. They sent the letter to him. He turned up at my office today and shouted at me in front of everyone, amma.'

She felt her face redden.

'I'm sorry, Appa. Did you retrieve the letter from him?'

'He refused to let me have it.'

Everyone in Jamshedpur knew that man, Swaminathan. He was an astrologer. He made predictions. He also took on the responsibility for all the pujas, festivals and celebrations among the Tamil people in town. He took charge of collecting all donations and giving accounts. It was said that when his mother died, the first thing he did was to send his wife to remove the jewellery from her body.

One day he actually turned up at their house. It was a direct attack.

He made for her mother, 'What is this, Amma, have you no idea about bringing up a girl properly? The boy is an utter innocent. It seems she hangs on to him like a *pisaasu*, and wanders about everywhere with him. It seems the whole town is laughing at them.'

He turned to her. 'Get on with leading a decent and correct life. Leave off enticing the neighbouring boys. I'll see to it that you won't be able to hold your head up in this town. Just watch it.'

'You get out of this house, first of all,' her mother told him, driving him out.

The letter went into the hands of every Tamil family in Jamshedpur. It reached all of them, but never Kadir. Eventually, it must have ended up among the waste paper in some Tamil household.

She had revealed all her doubts in that letter, all the anguish she felt.

'Of course I need you, and the closeness of you. That kiss on that terrace is still wet on my lips. The touch of your hand on my smouldering body does indeed set it aflame. But it seems to me that as far as I'm concerned, our meeting has happened too late, whereas on your part, it is too soon. I have travelled many miles. You, though, are still within the womb of your family. You don't quite know how to come out of it. But you have to make your way outside, first of all. You can find a life of your own only after that.

I feel as if I am being tied down, hand and foot.

Sometimes I wonder if these feelings which well up within me and my body belong to an instant that will simply float away.'

It was as if everything was blasted apart by an earthquake. When the Emergency was declared by the central government, Arangannal made the decision to follow the politics of the extreme left. Amudan sought to change his job. Kadir asked for a transfer and went to Chandigarh.

After the storm died down, Kadir left for the United States. They planned that before he went away, they would all go down together, to Amudan's house in Kanchipuram.

~

They spread their mats and lay down to sleep. The early part of the night went by silently. Then the cow called out a few times, 'Mmaa'. She heard the creak of the swing in the kuudam, as it moved. Noises of the calf, running about. Kadir lay on a mat within an arm's reach. He slept with his arms crossed over his chest. She wanted to reach across and touch him. But she pushed away her desire. Let all that remain truly at an end. When she had fallen asleep at last she felt that wet roughness against her cheek. She shivered. When she opened her eyes, she saw the calf bending over her with wondering eyes, licking her cheek. As if it were gentling her. Its tongue felt cold against her cheek. Like a wet kiss.

~

Kadir's letter arrived a few days after she returned home.

'I don't know why Udayan hesitated to tell me that you were living together. It gives me great satisfaction that he was with you for ten years. I still feel his loss.

40

He might have thought that he never achieved anything in his life. But what have others achieved, other than the achievement of staying alive?

I continue to live in this country although I find fault with its politics and culture. But I don't have the will to return to India either. I think this will be a lifelong struggle for me.

You have your feet firmly planted in some place, somewhere. As for me, I feel as though beneath my feet there is nothing but air. I am cursed, like Trisanku, neither to hold firm, nor to fall. Do you remember a poem by Atmanam, which says, what I need is a place where I can be. It strikes me it was written for me, or for people like me who cannot put down substantial roots.

I think one day I will die during a car journey on an American highway. You might come to hear of it. Or you might not.

On our last car journey together, you stroked the back of my neck with fingers that had been holding an ice-cream cone. Thanks. I shivered at that moment. That touch felt cool. Like a wet kiss . . .'

~

Even before Kadir's letter arrived, she had written to him in detail about Udayan's death.

'I don't know entirely, why he made that decision. But I can make a guess. About a month before Udayan's death, Mukund's health worsened greatly. He could not even get out of bed. Udayan was with him constantly. One night, when he was in great pain, Mukund apparently asked him, "If anything happens to me, don't abandon Akka. Stay with her." Udayan was stunned. Apparently he wept and said, "Mukund, I am not capable of taking on any sort of responsibility. I am only a vagabond, a bird of passage. Please don't threaten me."

'Do you remember that painting by Edward Munch? A face frozen with terror. I saw that look on Udayan. A look as if he had gazed upon death, close up. One evening, when I came home, I found him looking for Sampath's novel, *Idaiveli, Interval.*

'Even when he invited me to visit his sister's house in Bangalore, with him, he hadn't decided anything, I believe.

'Perhaps he might have thought about it. In his diary, there was only a quotation from *Tirumandiram*. There was only that.

"If a kuyil lays its eggs
in the nest of a crow
the crow rears its chicks
tirelessly, in good faith.
Even so,
without movement, without direction,
without cause or reason,
as if in delusion
the body is cared for."

'The second day after we arrived in Bangalore, he fell into the well in the back garden of his sister's large house. Someone screamed, and before I could reach him, he had been lifted out. I went to him, lifted his dripping hand and laid it against my cheek. It seemed then as if he was still alive. It felt cold. Like a wet kiss . . .'

Journey 6

She began to wonder whether they lived in one of Mumbai's apartment blocks, or in a fortress. Within a few weeks, the nameplates in the foyer had been removed. If you went up to the terrace, you would find, strewn about, broken soda bottles and sharp stones, small enough to be held in the palm of a hand. They claimed it was in aid of self-defence. One evening, about a week ago, a motley crowd tried to enter the building, shouting and screaming. Sticks, tridents, orange-coloured flags, etc. held in hand. They called out every Muslim family who lived in the block, by name, and demanded that they should all go downstairs. They were equipped with a list of all these families. The Nepalese guards tried to close the entrance doors. As soon as the police van sounded in the distance, the mob hurried away along the lanes nearby. The soda bottles and the sharp stones were the result of that event.

Barbed-wire fences appeared along the outside walls of the sea-facing block, as if establishing a boundary. Every day, the sunset bore barbed-wire marks across its

43

face. Occasionally, a rubber ball thrown by one of the children who lived in the building—it could never be determined who, exactly—fell across the barbed wire on to the adjacent sandy sea beach. Some of these balls rolled away swiftly, into the sea. Streaked with sand, red, green and blue balls lay scattered all along the beach. Some of them just paddled in the water. None of the children ever went downstairs in search of their ball. They never laid claim to any. The coloured balls lay about, orphaned.

It was during that seething time that Mumtaz called. She asked if she could help move Aslam Khan Saheb to another house. He was in a bad way, she said, after he had taken part in the Republic Day procession calling for peace and religious harmony. When asked what exactly the matter was, she replied, 'Exhaustion.' She said he needed further chemotherapy. When he spoke that day, his exhaustion was indeed apparent. Yes, it showed on his face as he stood there at the road junction, having walked past burnt-out houses, cars that were like brinjals thrust into a fire, and individuals who touched him with trembling hands and tried to speak to him. 'What can I say,' he began in Hindi. He repeated, 'Tell me, what can I say? I have spoken so many times; I have said it in so many ways. But nobody is willing to listen. I received two letters yesterday. One said, "You are a traitor who doesn't know the Qu'ran. May you rot and die." The other said, "You are an enemy of the Hindus. You are a parasite. May you burn and die. We shall watch and rejoice." I don't know which of these wishes will be fulfilled. I don't know by whose wish all this is happening. Who is it that wants to burn a car complete with three people in it? Who desires children to watch their parents die? Who wants parents to watch their daughters being raped? Tell me my friends. What thread did we fail to hold on to . . .'

He spoke in this way for an hour. The crowd was spellbound.

It was arranged that he would stay with a friend who lived close by the hospital which was near Shivaji Park, Mumtaz said. This friend lived in a large mansion. There was a little summer house in their back garden which would be appropriate. The friend was very insistent Aslam Khan Saheb should move there. He would be sending his car at two o'clock. Khan Saheb was anxious she should accompany him. He was asking to see her, constantly.

As soon as she agreed to go, Mumtaz told her that her neighbour's son, Abdul, would be waiting for her outside Jogeshwari station, and that he would bring her to the house, on his scooter. She should not take the bus or auto or any other means of transport.

Abdul was waiting for her, as arranged, outside Jogeshwari station. He took her on his scooter to Khan Saheb's place. Supporting Aslam Khan Saheb on either side, she and Mumtaz helped him into the car, and told the driver to go very slowly. He sat there, looking out of the window. He didn't speak a word. He was holding Mumtaz's hand very tightly in his. When she took his other hand in both hers, he turned and looked at her fondly. He said he was giving her a lot of trouble. She scolded him for being so formal with her, even after they had known each other for so many years. He laughed then. By the time she had settled them into the Shivaji Park house, making sure they had all they needed, and then set off at a good pace to catch her train at Dadar station, it was all of five o'clock. Usually, at that time, the crowds were unbearable. That is why Mumtaz had insisted she go by train this time. The crowds would be dense. They would embrace her. Push her. Protect her. She could fold the crowds about her, like a blanket.

But on that day, she didn't have that shield. Yes, there were people about. But not the crowds that usually filled the station to overflowing. As soon as the train arrived, she climbed into the women's compartment. The express train usually arrived at platform two. There would be a crowd there. She found a seat right next to the exit.

She got down at Andheri station, climbed up the stairs hurriedly and had just reached the overbridge, when the shouting started. People were running about all over the bridge.

A voice screamed, 'Don't go west, towards the mosque.'

Another voice yelled, 'Avoid the east; don't go towards the bus stand.'

Heavy footsteps thudded past. People jostled about, in distress. She found herself shoved towards platform one. From where she was, on the bridge, she could see platform one beneath her. Broken soda-water bottles were flung about everywhere. And stones. A broken soda-water bottle stood upright in a corner. Its jagged edge was tinged with red. Pale red blood lay spilt all around it. It hit the eyes like a still-life painting.

A sudden shouting. An older man, bearded and wearing a lungi was running between the railway lines along platform one. Four or five youths were pursuing him. They reached out and pulled at his *lungi*, taking no notice of his pleading. Left naked from his waist down, the man crouched down on his haunches immediately.

They rolled him over and down. Their arms rose, holding sticks, soda bottles and cycle chains.

She heard someone sobbing, and turned to see a five-year-old boy. Before they lowered their arms she leaned the little boy against herself and covered his eyes with her hands.

The old man's voice rose in a scream and rang out in a heart-rending cry, '*Bachaav, bachaav,* (Help! Help!)'

She could not cover the boy's ears.

A thousand words, one life

When Kamakshi found herself pregnant for the third time, she was somewhat shaken. She did not know at what impulsive moment, during which upsurge of emotion, her womb could have received the seed.

The Second World War was going on at the time. There was severe rationing. Life in Bombay afforded them little chance of savings. A household managed by carrying bags of wheat to the Panjabi family that lived three floors above them and receiving their rice in exchange. It was a life which avoided scarcity. A life that avoided luxury too. There were no objects in their house which were in the least bit showy. She wondered if this third pregnancy was itself an unnecessary luxury.

She tried various potions during the next two months: green papaya, powdered sesame seeds, crushed henna leaves dissolved in water. The foetus was like a stone, unmoved by any of this. After a while, she gave up all such attempts. But a fear lurked in the corner of her mind: in what shape would this foetus finally arrive, having resisted all attempts to shift it?

Her father wrote from Coimbatore. She had a fragile body. She would find it very difficult to manage this pregnancy as well as taking care of her two older children. She should return to her parents' house in Coimbatore, as early as her sixth month. Her husband gave his consent. The eldest child, a boy, was just coming up to his Christmas holidays. The school authorities agreed that it would not matter greatly if he could not attend classes for a month or so. The second, a girl, was a chatterbox. She came away, having informed her teacher, 'My Amma is going to have a baby. I'm going to Coimbatore with her.'

Her younger sister, Gauri, also arrived in Coimbatore, from Chennai. She too was expecting her third. Kamakshi's father had only recently been transferred to Coimbatore, from Kovilpatti. The house was in R.S. Puram. It was a quiet place, without a fly or crow to be seen anywhere near. The next house was a short distance away.

As soon as she arrived in Coimbatore, she felt a huge relief. Her older two played with Gauri's children, in the garden or in the street. After herself and Gauri, there were eight other younger siblings. The last of them, a little sister, was only three. The house was animated and lively, full of all the children.

Their mother was full of care and concern for Gauri and herself. She would massage them gently with oil and give them baths. She would make Kamakshi lie down and spread out her long hair upon a basket upturned over a vessel of smoking frankincense. Gauri's hair was short. Their mother would make her sit up and untangle it with her fingers. Even at her relatively young age, their mother always had a *tevaram* on her lips. She was always singing softly, '*Kaadalaagi kasindu kannir malgi*', 'Melting

49

with love, eyes brimming' or *'Mandiramaavadu niiru'*, 'Magical is the sacred ash'. As Kamakshi lay there, leaning her head against the frankincense basket and gazing up at the ceiling from which the huge rings of the swing were suspended, she could not feel at all the weight of her stomach. She felt as if she were an *apsara*, floating in a world of smoke. It was as if Bombay and its severe regulations, and all the attempts she had made to abort the baby, belonged far away, in a distant world.

Her husband was adamant that the baby should only be born in a hospital. He was terrified of a home birth after hearing about an incident which happened in a household nearby. Customarily, the much experienced older women in the family took charge of any childbirth themselves. The barber's wife would come only to cut the umbilical cord. Or if the women knew how to do it, they would attend to that business as well. Kamakshi's great-aunt Rajammal was a woman who had delivered many babies. She could do everything. She bought clean, new razor blades with her own money, and kept them in a small brass box. She would set off with her brass box, at whatever time she was summoned, and to any family that needed her. However difficult the delivery, she wasn't frightened. Once when she arrived at one of the hutments, she found the baby in a breach position. Without hesitating a moment, Rajammal Paatti put her hand through the birth passage and turned the baby.

As soon as she had cut the umbilical cord she would set off home. The family would attend to bathing the new mother themselves; in some households the washerwoman did it. As for Rajammal Paatti, she went her way, after advising them to splash plenty of hot water on the young woman as they bathed her, and reminding them to bind her stomach tightly with strips of cloth. After every delivery, whoever the girl, she had a bath as soon as she returned home, and then sent to the new mother a small brass box full of the special *legiyam* that she made and stored away, from time to time. Even if a midwife attended to the actual delivery, people turned to Rajammal Paatti for the legiyam.

But the irony was that Rajammal herself had no children. Nobody had ever seen a smile on her husband's face. He never addressed Rajammal by name. 'Ask that barren prostitute to come here,' he'd say. The story went that just once, when he was sitting in the thinnai playing cards with his friends and summoned her loudly in this way, she came outside, placed a *kuuja* of coffee and four silver tumblers near him, and asked, in front of everyone, 'Who is the barren one here, you or I?' She stood quietly, asked her question, then went inside in haste. It seemed that after that, he stopped talking to her altogether.

Rajammal came to Kovilpatti from Satyamangalam, to attend on Kamakshi, for her two earlier deliveries. But now, Rajammal wasn't there. One day she delivered a baby in her usual way, came home, sent the legiyam and fell asleep. She never woke up. The baby girl she delivered last was named Rajammal in memory of her. Every child she touched became part of her dynasty. If a man creates his dynasty through his seed, how many families does a woman create through those she touches in this way? Families that are not confined by the direct relationships of caste, religion, blood, status. In Satyamangalam, a girl named Rajammal must be running about. Would she remember Rajammal's touch? The touch of those hands which held her even before she reached this earth? Would she remember any of that? How can we say which of the events that make up history are remembered, and which forgotten? History is made up of so many silences.

Kamakshi's eyes would close as she lay there, head against the frankincense basket, lost in her thoughts. But her mother would insist on waking her up. 'You mustn't fall asleep after an oil massage and bath. You will get a headache,' she'd say. She would wake her up, plait her hair for her, loosely, and bring bowls of hot *rava-kesari* for both the young women, made with milk and semolina and dripping with ghee. Later, she and Gauri would sit on the thinnai and chatter away as they picked stones out of the rice, or chopped the vegetables.

It was during those times too, that they often talked about the terrible event which made them both agree to the decision that they should have their babies only at the hospital.

Their parents heard about that incident a couple of months after they settled in Coimbatore. An old woman who lived a few doors away spoke to their mother about it. When the old woman's second daughter, who lived in a neighbouring town, became pregnant, her mother-in-law and she attended to her delivery. Neither of the older women realized that the girl was carrying twins. When the girl's labour appeared to continue, even after the first baby had been delivered, this lady voiced her suspicion that there might be yet another baby in the girl's womb. But the mother-in-law proceeded to bandage the girl's stomach tightly, proclaiming firmly, 'There have been no twins in our family, ever.' The child's death poisoned the girl's entire body, and she, too, gave up her life.

'We killed our girl ourselves, amma. The life inside her was not able to come out. We went and bound up a life that was about to be free. It was only when the bandages were loosened that we realized what had happened. After that, by the time we rushed her to the hospital, before mother and child could be separated, both died.' The old woman repeated her story to their mother several times, lamenting loudly. It might have been an error that happened very rarely. All the same, the very thought of it made them shudder from the depths of their stomachs. Rajammal Paatti's gently warm hands weren't there to give them courage. So it was that they decided it must be the hospital for them.

It looked as if Gauri and she would go into labour more or less at the same time. Her third child decided to arrive at a time when their father was on tour. She had just had her evening meal, washed her hands and popped a betel into her mouth when she felt that stabbing pain at the middle of her back. Six years had passed since the birth of her second. She had forgotten the pain. For a second she was shocked, and then she realized what it was. Before she could call out to her mother, there it was again. Her mother was taken by surprise, just a little. Then, she called the gardener, Velucchami, and sent him off to fetch a rickshaw. She decided that Velucchami's wife, Mutthamma should keep Gauri company. As soon as the rickshaw arrived she helped Kamakshi into it, and climbed in after her. The rickshawman left for the hospital, pulling the vehicle gently and without haste. Yet each turn of the wheel seem to go right across her waist. Her mother's cheek, smelling of turmeric, was close to her face. There was no movement along the street. Street lights shone here and there. When she leaned her head against her mother's shoulder, and looked upwards, she could see the moon very clearly. A journey that felt endless. It would always stay in her mind, she reflected.

As soon as they reached the hospital, her mother asked the rickshaw to wait, and went inside with her. She made Kamakshi lie down on a bed. The hospital was dusty and full of rubbish. Mosquitoes swarmed about. The doctor who examined her pronounced that she would give birth only the next day. Kamakshi told her mother to go home, and to return in the morning. Her mother found the hospital uncongenial. She decided to go home.

At about four in the morning, the pain became much more forceful. In the delivery room, the nurse spoke sharply to her, for no reason at all. She had moaned softly, without even raising her voice. At once the nurse fell on her. 'What's all this moaning and groaning for,' she rapped out. At about four thirty, as she thrust her neck and head back and gave a strong push, her gaze fell directly on the window; a single star filled her eyes. The baby fell against the crook of her thigh, bringing it warmth. The words, 'A baby girl' sounded, as if from afar. In an instant there was a loud cry. Then she sank into oblivion.

When she came to, briefly, she could see that both she and the baby were covered in a white sheet stained with shit. She called out softly to the nurse and said, 'Please change this sheet.' Once more she was overcome by weariness.

In the morning her mother arrived with piping hot *kanji* made of rava. As Kamakshi drank the kanji, her mother examined the baby.

'Kamu, she is the very same colour as your sister-in-law.'

'As dark as that?'

'It's as if her whole body is covered with moles. Just take a look.'

'Amma, please see if her arms, legs, ears and everything are all in place.'

Her mother's face darkened. 'Why? Did you go take some sort of potion?' she asked.

When she nodded, her mother said, 'You wretch . . .' and proceeded to stroke the baby's fingers, her limbs, the flaps of her ears, and all her body. Nothing wrong whatever.

'Nothing at all wrong, Kamu.'

'Thank goodness for that much. If there were something wrong, and being a girl at that, where could I have gone and knocked my head?'

'What does she lack? She is going to be exactly like her maternal grandmother.'

'I'll give her the same name as you,' Kamakshi said, Ranganayaki.

'Today is Friday. An auspicious day. You are going to become very wealthy through her.' She added the good fortune of Friday to the name.

Sriranganayaki.

The name was shortened to Nayaki, even before Kamakshi brought her home. Nayaki did not care for her mother's milk. She refused stubbornly to drink it. She lay silent, while the boy baby, born to Gauri the following week, screamed through the night. If she was given a bottle, she drank the milk. Otherwise, she didn't make the slightest noise. Sometimes, Mutthamma would carry Nayaki to her home at the bottom of the garden. Mutthamma had a two-month-old baby. For some reason, whenever Mutthamma picked up Nayaki, Nayaki would develop a sudden desire for milk. She would turn her head towards her breasts and begin to whimper for milk. Sometimes Mutthamma would feed her own baby at one breast, and give her other breast to Nayaki, who by this time would be clamouring and throwing her limbs about. When she was done, she would lie there, quietly smiling. Once Kamakshi came to the bottom of the garden to see. 'Mutthamma,' she said, 'Nayaki doesn't care for my milk, she likes only yours.' As long as they stayed in Coimbatore, Mutthamma fed Nayaki at least once a day.

After three months, her father put them on the train to Bombay. There were twenty-five packages including *appalam*, various spice powders and prepared condiments. Gifts from the bridal home, sent by her mother. A Singer sewing machine. ('You have given up music, now at least keep this. What is in the heart has to come out in one form or another. Otherwise, you'll just go mad.') That was put in the luggage van. Her father accompanied her as far as Arakonam, and helped her to change trains. A telegram had already gone off to Bombay.

The train arrived in Bombay. She couldn't see her husband. Fear seized her heart. All the same she began to think hard as to how best she should reach home. First of all she made the older boy and girl climb down from the train. She placed the three-month-old baby in the boy's arms and told him to hold her very carefully. She made the girl stand close up to her brother. The little girl, for her part, also put an arm around the baby.

Then, with the help of a coolie, she brought down all twenty-five pieces of luggage. She ran to the luggage van and collected the sewing machine.

She came outside the station with everything, and negotiated the fare home, on two Victoria coaches. They arrived home, the bigger pieces of luggage with herself, the baby and the little girl in one coach, the boy and the rest of the luggage in the other. The total fare came to a rupee: eight annas for each coach.

When they reached home, she found that her husband was just about to set off to his office. The telegram had never reached him. He was totally surprised by her arrival. All of them went inside.

Nayaki arrived, too. She was laid in a corner. The husband did not pick her up in his arms. That night he complained: she was dark-skinned, she was not chubby; she was a girl. He did not say that they should take the baby to a studio and have her photographed. Neither did Kamakshi think of it. Her return to a life of coping with wartime shortage, left no time for anything else.

When Kamakshi's younger brother visited them in Bombay, Nayaki was already four and sucking her thumb ceaselessly. Her brother insisted stubbornly that he should take the child to a studio and have her photographed. He claimed that she looked exactly like the film star, Nargis. So Kamakshi made a beautiful dress for the child. The Parsi woman living next door subscribed to a women's weekly which came from London. Kamakshi borrowed the magazine and copied one of the children's dresses modelled there. A cotton material, patterned densely with flowers. It had a full skirt and a bib front, with decorative shoulder straps which crossed over at the back. A white blouse with puff sleeves. When she wore it, Nayaki was as pretty as a doll. She had tightly curling hair.

In the studio photo that her uncle arranged, Nayaki looked straight ahead of her, slightly bewildered. She looked a little shy as she stood there, the thumb she always sucked held together with her forefinger, in a circle.

At the age of four, Nayaki loved her thumb above everything. Because it had been sucked constantly, it looked somewhat pale and was worn smooth at the knuckle. As soon as anyone spoke sharply to her, that thumb would be popped into her mouth. She would sit down and lean against the wall, finger in her mouth.

She first began to draw with a slate pencil. She made many pictures using the coloured crayons belonging to the Bengali woman who lived next door. She would lay a blue oil crayon against white paper, press it down, and roll it across. Waves would form across one part of the paper. As soon as she finished, she would go and show Kamakshi her picture. Kamakshi would very likely be fast asleep, tired out from her morning's chores. The two older ones would have just gone back to school after their midday meal. Sometimes, she would glance at the pictures and say wearily, 'Yes, yes, now off you go.' The paper would be tossed in a corner, and end up on the dust heap. Nayaki would go off and draw another picture.

On the advice of her mother, Kamakshi began to massage Nayaki's stick-like limbs with castor oil before bathing her, in the hope of strengthening and filling them out. She would smear oil all over the child and then massage her firmly. There would be a Ramayana story at the same time, to stop her from crying. Always it was the story of the birth of Rama.

'A Gandharvan came out of the fire-pit bringing a silver bowl full of milk *payasam*. He gave it to all three of them: Kausalya, Sumitra and Kaikeyi. So all three of the queens drank that payasam. After that, some days later, a baby came and lay down in each of their stomachs.'

'Amma, did you too drink payasam, Amma, before I came into your stomach?'

'Payasam? Of course I did.'

'Out of a silver bowl?'

'Of course. It was a beautiful silver bowl. You know the bowl in which I place flowers for the puja? That very same one.'

It was a finely worked bowl. Creepers rose from its base and spread all over it, covering it with flowers and leaves and fruit.

'Mm. And then?'

'You know, I drank that payasam? It was a payasam in which the milk was boiled down and boiled down. A payasam in which the rice and the milk were so well mixed and mingled, it melted in my mouth. I drank it and drank it and made you grow. Then I went to Coimbatore.'

By this time she would mix the *shiyakkai* and place it on the child's hair. Nayaki had to shut her eyes tightly to stop the shiyakkai from falling into them. Coimbatore would begin to take shape within her closed eyes.

Amma would describe the hospital: a palace such as the one where the sons of Dasaratha were born. A hospital that had just been built, brand new. A building as freshly white as tumbai flowers. Inside, the walls covered in pastel colours. New iron bedsteads. Shining white sheets. Window curtains patterned in tiny flowers in rose and violet. Nurses and doctors all in white, like angels. At dawn, Nayaki was born, surrounded by these angels. The auspicious goddess of the family was born.

Nayaki would emerge from the bathroom, a towel wrapped around herself, given new life. In her imagination, a princess.

~

She pressed the red button, and then said to Nayaki, 'Go ahead.' The journalist was interviewing artists in order to write about their life and art.

Nayaki began, 'I was born during the Second World War . . .'

~

Everything had to be contained within a thousand words. Artists, after all, once they started speaking could go on for ever. So each was allowed a thousand words. Only a thousand words. Nayaki had spoken about her birth and how her mother had described the hospital to her, imagining it to be a palace; she told it as a story. She said that although her mother was not an artist by profession, she was indeed an artist. She said that the story of her birth was a good example of the selectiveness of memory, and how the events selected by the memory become changed. She ended that section with the words, 'I never tried to find out what that hospital was really like. Nor did I enquire about any of the other details. It is not that I cannot face the truth. But that imaginary version is my mother's gift to me. It has the warmth of the fine fibres lining a bird's nest. A safeguard. I can't tell whether she told it for that reason. And it isn't important anyway. Because we live this life through the real and the imagined, memory and forgetfulness.'

That section alone went on for over ten minutes. Once transcribed, it would run to two or three pages. The journalist, who went about her task meticulously, wrote down only her date of birth and pressed the button to fast forward the tape.

Journey 7

The moment they set foot into Bandra station, from where Chandrakant was to set off on his journey, they were engulfed by a jostling crowd. Some people were running, shoving their way through the crowd. Others ambled along, blocking the passageways. There were the customary long queues at the ticket windows. Fights, scuffles, queue-jumping. Coolies calling out to people to get out of their way.

The Delhi train was standing on the platform. Chandrakant handed her his suitcase and went off to buy her platform ticket. It was when she stood back a little, and moved to one side, that her gaze fell on the woman. She sat on the floor, close by the wall, right by the entrance to the platform, surrounded by a trunk, two cloth bundles, a baby reaching up to suckle, and a six-year-old boy looking about him and star-gazing. The baby, smacked a couple of times on its bottom, started to wail. She pulled at the boy and gave him a couple of cuffs on the head, as well, for good measure. He plonked himself down on the trunk, crying loudly. Having made both her children weep, the woman's own eyes began to fill. She wiped her eyes and lifted her head. That was when she must have seen her.

'Mausiji . . ., Mausiji . . .' she called.

She went up to the woman and asked, 'What's the matter?'

'When does the train to Mathura arrive?'

'When does it arrive? It's standing on the platform already. Look, there it is, right in front of you. Where exactly do you want to go?'

'It's a small village, next to Mathura. Is there another train after this one, Mausiji?'

'Why can't you go on this one? Haven't you bought a ticket or what?'

'No, I want to go on the next one. When is it due?'

'This is the last train. The next one will leave only tomorrow.'

The woman clasped her children to herself and was silent.

Meanwhile, Chandrakant had returned. He asked what was going on. When she explained, he too went up to the woman and tried to reason with her. When she gave him a cursory and non-committal answer, he turned away. 'Come, let's go,' he said, 'there seems to be some sort of problem there.'

They entered the platform, located his coach and he climbed in immediately. She went in with him, saw him settled in a seat by the window, his suitcase stowed away, and then climbed out and stood outside. They talked of this and that until the train made ready to leave. As it began pulling out, she spoke urgently, 'Make sure to eat properly. Don't drink too much.' He called back as he smiled and waved, 'Let me give you the same advice.'

He held to the unshakeable belief that alcohol was the best medicine for all the ailments of the body or the mind. It was a true panacea for everything. The brandy bottle made its appearance if either of them produced the slightest snuffle or cough. 'How can you survive without your medicine?' he'd say. And she would agree. He had a long list of remedies: rum and hot water for a fever; a Bloody Mary consisting of vodka and tomato juice for a cloudy mind, or a screwdriver of vodka and orange juice. Or Chandrakant's special discovery, vodka in watermelon juice, a slit chilli floating on top. On cheerful days, wine, to kindle even more cheer. Champagne for celebration. And Glenfiddich malt whisky for a special and unexpected celebration.

To her family, brought up on proverbs such as 'Drink leads to utter ruin', and accustomed to the overacting in Indian films, where a single mouthful of alcohol is followed immediately by a drunken stagger, Chandrakant's beliefs about drink were absolutely shocking. It was the first time they encountered such a culture shock. They insisted that she 'reform' their son-in-law. After she told them that it was part of his culture, that the women in his community also drank alcohol with pleasure, and gave them a history lesson about how, fifty years ago, the women in the villages of the north would brew toddy themselves, and sell it in big pots from their houses, her parents stopped talking about it entirely.

As she set off homeward, smiling a little, she was stopped by the woman who called out again, 'Mausiji, Mausiji!' When she turned round, she saw the woman, beckoning her. She went up to her once more and asked, 'Now what?'

'Mausiji, please hold him for a bit. I'll just go to the toilet,' she said, holding out the baby. The baby reached towards her, smiling, as if he was long familiar with her.

The woman said to the baby fondly, 'Ei Kishen, you mustn't give Nani-mausi any trouble.'

Nani-mausi! She had been conferred grandmother status in an instant.

'Mausiji, please keep an eye on my luggage as well,' the woman said, taking the older boy by the hand, ready to go.

'What's your name?'

'Rupmati. This boy is Arjun.'

'Very well. Go then, and come back very quickly.'

The baby wore only a shirt. She opened her bag with one hand, took out a hand towel, wrapped it about the baby's waist, and settled him on her arm. He slithered about, refusing to stay still. He laid his head against her shoulder as if it were his right, and grabbed hold of the chain she wore at her neck, and pulled at it. He thrust his fingers through her hair. He laughed at something or the other, dribbling the while, then he rubbed his face against her.

'Look here, I'm not your Nani. Don't get too cheeky,' she said to him, with a tight expression.

He clapped his hands and laughed, reaching out for her hair, and rumpling it.

The crowds all around them kept rushing to and fro.

It was all of ten or fifteen minutes before Rupmati appeared at a distance. By that time she was quite tired of dealing with the baby's antics.

She handed him over, as soon as Rupmati came up. Rupmati took the baby, but stood there, looking at her.

'The last train has left. What will you do now?'

'If a man's wife leaves the house at eight in the morning, and doesn't appear again, shouldn't he come and look for her, Mausiji? I've been here since nine. Nobody has come to find me. Now I have to go to Mathura, and then catch a bus to my village . . . '

'Who do you have there?'

'My Bhaisaheb, Bhabhiji and Bavuji. I don't have a mother . . . My village is very far away.'

For some reason, she remembered Nirmala Putul's poem in Santali. A poem in which a girl addresses her father:

Baba,
Don't get me married at a place so far
that you can only come to see me
by selling your goats

Don't arrange a marriage for me at a place
where only gods live, not men
Let it not be in a town
where there are no woods
nor mountains nor rivers.
Most definitely
not in a place where cars fly
faster than thoughts
Or where there are high buildings
and huge shops

Please don't seek a bridegroom for me
in a house where the dawn does not break

to the cock crowing in the front yard,
nor in a house where you cannot see the sun
setting beyond the mountains
from the backyard . . .

Don't hand me over to a man
who has never so far planted a tree nor sown a field
who has not carried other people's burdens
whose hand cannot even write the word, 'hand' . . .

If you must get me married,
let it be at a place
to which you can walk in the morning
and return at sunset.
If I weep by the shores of the river
you should hear it at the further shore
and come to me quickly . . .

Rupmati stood in front of her, confused and dazed. She looked as if she hadn't eaten throughout the day. Outside the station, it was beginning to darken.

'Wait a little, I'll be back,' she told her, and hurried away, taking Arjun by the hand. At the canteen she bought two *vada-pav*, the food that was for Bombayites the chief means of appeasing hunger. She also bought a plastic cup full of milk and a packet of biscuits. She gave Arjun all the packages to carry, then bought three cups of tea which she took in both her hands, proceeding to walk carefully without spilling any of the hot liquid. Arjun walked by her side, holding the cup of milk and the other packets with great care.

Rupmati and Arjun sat down on the trunk. Rupmati fed the baby with the biscuits and milk, and set him down. She herself sipped her tea and watched the mother and son enjoy the inch-thick pav buns stuffed with potato. Rupmati looked as if she was twenty-two or twenty-three years old. Large black eyes. Thick, well-defined eyebrows. Her hair looked reddish, as if it hadn't been oiled. A nylon sari in a deep green colour. Yellow *choli*.

When she finished eating, Rupmati threw the paper plates and cups into the rubbish bin, picked up Kishen once more, and came up to her.

'Well, Rupmati? What have you decided to do?'

'Look here, Mausiji, he drives his auto all day, doesn't give me a penny, comes home drunk, wakes up at seven and demands his breakfast immediately. How is it possible? There is no kerosene in the house. No pav. No milk. No tea dust. My *saasuma* had already left for work. It would take at least an hour for her to finish giving oil massage and baths to the newly delivered babies and their mothers she attends to. She usually has her food in one of their houses. Arjun and Kishen can only look to me. I have to get Kishen ready for school. There isn't even wheat flour in the house to make rotis for his lunch-box. When I told him there was nothing in the house, my husband kicked things about in the house, gave me a couple of blows for my pains and left. What's more, he told me to get out of the house. Go back to your parents' house, he said. I got angry as well. I went off directly, and sold my earrings. I gathered up my things and set off. But look, they don't care at all. Not one of them has come looking for me.'

'How would they know you are here? They might be looking for you somewhere nearer the house.'

She got the impression that a couple of bystanders were staring at Rupmati.

'Anyway you can't stay here through the night. It won't do you any good.'

'Then where can I go?'

'Look here, how can he order you to leave the house? Isn't it your house as well? Now, you just go back. Put your trunk in the front of the house and settle yourself there. Let everyone see you. Let them question him. Won't your sassurji say anything to him?'

'He himself is a drunkard.'

'Fine. What about your saasuma?'

'Oh, her? How can one say whose side she will take?'

The trunk was raised on to Arjun's head. The cloth bundles climbed up to Rupmati's head. Kishen at her hip.

She came outside the railway station, and stopped an auto, and brought it over to a side. It was apparent at once, that the autorickshaw man was from Uttar Pradesh. Ninety per cent of the autos and taxis in Mumbai were owned by people of that region.

'Where to?' she asked Rupmati.

'Malvani'

'Malvani? It's quite a long way from here by road. How did you get here this morning?'

'We took a bus to Madh Island, then a boat to Versova village, then a bus again to the station.'

Motor boats plied near the fishing area, owned by the fishermen. The fares were cheap. They made the sea-crossing in five minutes. By road it was circuitous route. It would take a whole hour.

'The last boat must have left already. Well, well, never mind. Come along,' she said, piling the luggage into the auto. She told them to climb in. The trunk took up most of the space, so they had to huddle close to each other.

She explained to the auto driver the way along the main road and how to get to the link road. Then she said, 'Look here, this woman comes from your own part of the country. If you go along the Malad road, the fare should come to a hundred rupees, or a hundred and ten. I'll give you two hundred. Will you take them home safely?'

He was doubtful. 'Auntyji, it looks as if there's been a fight or something in their family. Suppose when I take her there, they turn around and beat me up?' He went on, after a while, 'Why don't you come as well? I'll take you home afterwards.'

'Mausiji, Bhaisaheb is right, isn't he? Why don't you come with us,' Rupmati joined in. Arjun, opening his mouth for the first time, added, 'Nani-Mausi, please come.'

It seemed she had become their grandmother for all time. Kishen, for good measure, smiled at her, displaying his tiny teeth like rice grains. She hesitated for a moment.

The auto driver said to Arjun, 'Beta, you come in front. Let Auntyji sit at the back.' Arjun jumped over the barrier railing, ran round to the front and sat down next to the driver. Rupmati pushed up further down the seat to make room while she climbed in and sat down with her legs across the trunk. The autorickshaw started to move.

The auto driver rang out, 'Bolo, Sri Ramchander ki jai! Pavana puthra Hanuman ki jai!' Perhaps he thought that without the help of the gods, he would not be able to

take them home. Whatever it was, Arjun joined in lustily
with 'Jai'.

The main road was always crowded with traffic. The
vehicles always went at high speed. The one consolation
was that they would not stop suddenly. She warned
the driver to be mindful of the children, and to go
carefully.

Rupmati, having railed at drunken husbands for a while,
laid her head on her 'Mausiji's' shoulder, and fell asleep.
So did Kishen, his legs stretched out against her lap.

As soon as they reached Malvani, she woke Rupmati
and asked her to direct the auto driver. But even before
that, Arjun had pointed out the way home. The auto
stopped at a neighbourhood of single-room dwellings.
They carried the trunk out with the auto driver's help
and put it down in front of Rupmati's house. Rupmati
sat down on it, with her children on either side of her.
Kishen leaned against his mother, still asleep. Gradually
the neighbours began to gather around.

In the courtyard, a man of between fifty to sixty years
sat on his rope-bed, smoking a *bidi* and refusing to look
at them.

Hearing them arrive, a young man burst outside.
Probably Rupmati's husband. He began to yell, 'You left
the house at eight in the morning, and you are back now,
are you? Where have you been?' Seeing the others there
he stopped short. Kishen woke up and began to cry.

One of the men standing among the crowd said, 'Don't
shout unnecessarily. This lady here has brought them
back.'

The young man saw her, and folded his hands in
respect and began his tale. 'Why should you take so much

trouble, Madam? This woman does not know how to behave decently. She'll go with anyone who invites her. Women like her deserve to be stamped on, good and hard. Which is just what I did.'

Several people in the crowd began to remonstrate with him. The auto driver said, 'Come on now, Auntyji.'

'If any woman dares to open her mouth in this house, she'll die. I mean it. If you want to say anything, then go and say it in your father's house. This is my house,' he went on shouting.

She was just about to step forward and say a couple of sharp words to him, but was stopped by a woman's voice from inside the house.

'Who is the drunkard shouting from my threshold?'

The voice was followed by the appearance of a woman of about fifty. She was, most certainly, Rupmati's mother-in-law. She came outside, picked up a bamboo cane from a corner, and addressed her son, 'Why, you dog, what makes you think this is your house? This is the house I acquired when I worked for the municipality, da. I paid good money and bought it. This house is in my name. What did you say? So women mustn't raise their voices in this house? We will do just that, da. I'll speak out, so will my daughter-in-law . . .'

Rupmati called out, 'Saasuma,' and began to weep loudly. Arjun ran up to his grandmother and hugged her, saying, 'Dadi . . .'

The cane she held in her hand was still raised 'You get drunk and make trouble, do you, you dog? I've been worrying and fretting since this morning; I must have asked where Rupmati has gone at least a hundred times. By God's grace she has come home safely. But you drunken pair, father and son, have to make a song and a dance about it. Get out, the pair of you. Let's see you march to the police station.' She struck the ground with her cane.

'What have I done?' the older man smoking his bidi, muttered.

The crowd egged the older woman on. 'That's right, give it to them!'

Some people explained to her, as she stood there watching, 'If you say things about women not behaving decently, the old lady tends to get furious.' She wondered if she were observing a drama that was enacted frequently.

The auto driver nagged her to get going.

At last, Rupmati's husband told his wife to get up and started to carry the trunk and the bundles inside. As he turned to go, Saasuma gave his feet a stinging blow with the cane. He screamed. When the old lady raised the cane once more, Rupmati caught her hand.

She went up to Rupmati and gave her a card with her name and address. She folded her hands in a namaskaram to the mother-in-law. She stroked Arjun's head and touched Kishen's cheek.

The auto driver had started the engine of his vehicle. Rupmati walked up to the auto with her, Kishen on her hip. She climbed in and sat down. She said to Rupmati, 'Your saasuma is a good lady.'

Rupmati put her head into the auto and whispered, 'She's been drinking today . . .'

When she turned around, she caught the auto driver's eyes in the mirror, looking at her. The vehicle started to move. The crowd dispersed, clearing the way.

Kailasam

The moment she began to watch a ghost serial on the TV, Kailasam began to judder violently. Accompanied by a loud sound that went 'diku-diku-dak diku-diku-dak'. Annoyed, she stood up, put on a pair of rubber chappals, went up to Kailasam and touched it. Stroked it. Kailasam showed no signs of subsiding. In the serial, the ghost pushed open the lid of its coffin, sat up and stared. The actor must have fancied himself as another Christopher Lee. The ghost glared. It was bald; its eyes gave out a yellow light. Kailasam shuddered incessantly. She put her arms around it and hugged it. 'Kailasam, Kailasam,' she said in a gentle voice. Kailasam only juddered the more, as if in a religious frenzy. She laid her cheek against it. 'Enough now, Kailasam', she said, 'pull yourself together.' It began to wind down, its 'dak dak' sounding more and more slowly. She gave it a fond pat and went back to her chair, continuing to watch her serial. The ugly ghost was wandering about now, looking for young girls, whose blood it wanted to suck.

She watched the serial without much interest. Why couldn't the ghost have been a bit younger? What sort of ghost was this, with a bald pate and paunch? Only female ghosts tended to be young and pretty, dressed in thin cotton saris, their undergarments showing through; they walked delicately, anklets tinkling; they even sang songs.

Kailasam had fallen silent. Kailasam was her refrigerator, bought in 1985. In the early years, there were no problems with it. At that time, it had no name either. But in the past ten years, the freezer compartment began to get iced up as if the Himalayan mountains had planted themselves inside it. She had never travelled to those parts. Yet in Mumbai, in the third storey of a building, which looked as if it were falling down, her refrigerator seemed to fill with ice peaks reminiscent of the holy places of pilgrimage which lay all along the Himalayas. Sometimes a single piece of ice, tightly frozen, stood upright at its centre, exactly like a Siva lingam. However many times the defrost button was pressed, it simply would not melt. Sometimes it had to be broken down and removed. But even after it was thrown into the sink, it would take a long time to melt. A lingam which refused to melt. After that the name 'Kailasam' was conferred ceremoniously on the refrigerator.

All their household goods had been given names. The cactus plant given to her by Dhananjayan was Dhanush. The creeper with tiny flat leaves was Megha.

The plant that mistook itself for a tree and had shot up so high—it was the first thing she set eyes on when she woke up—was Usha. The plant that was attempting to grow awkwardly, with crooked branches, was Vakkiran.

Jayan teased her one day, 'Why have you given men's names only to the plants with thorns or awkward shapes?'

This giving of names wasn't entirely at random, it struck her. Was there a connection between Kailasam, her refrigerator, and another Kailasam, perhaps? When she was a university research student, the students' hostel was in two sections. The rooms adjacent to the warden's house belonged to the women. The men students had the building opposite. Between the two were the dining hall, a common room with a TV, and a grassy lawn. It was by way of a diversion from the boredom of their constant research work that she and her friends started giving nicknames to the men students. At first these remained straightforward names such as 'Broomstick' and 'Matchbox'. Gradually they changed into names which held complex and hidden meanings. It was Professor Gulati who started them off on a long chapter of conferring names with thousands of insinuations. Gulati had just been married. Gunwant Kaur brought the news that his wife was deeply unsatisfied. He finished his business in a great hurry, before she could feel any pleasure, apparently. The doctor whom the Professor consulted was a distant relative of Gunwant's uncle. That evening they named Professor Gulati, 'Waterfall'.

Dipika's boyfriend, Sikander, had a room on the first floor of the building opposite the women's hostel. He would often send signals to Dipika, who was on the second floor. The windows of the women's rooms were curtained most of the time, or their shutters were closed. One morning Sudha banged on her door, urgently. When she opened it, Sudha said excitedly, 'Open your window.' Even before she could do so, Sudha herself flung open the shutters and called out, 'Look!' Beneath them on the first floor, Sikander's window was wide open. Sikander lay on his bed naked, his sheet at his feet. His long male member fell to one side. The first penis she had ever seen. It had been circumcised. Sudha said it was a first time for her, too, and ran to fetch her binoculars. The two of them gave the penis their serious attention. When they focused on just that part of his anatomy, it seemed like a small snake, detached from the rest of his body; a gentle snake which fell away from him this way and that as he moved in his sleep.

One by one the rest—excepting Dipika—came in, took a hurried look, and left. Quite unaware that he had become an object worthy of *darshan*, Sikander lay there, fast asleep. They named Sikander, 'Snake'. Sudha could sing beautifully. If ever Sikander came within sight, she would begin to murmur, 'Oh Cobra, coiled above Siva's hair.' She'd repeat the refrain, 'Dance Snake! Play and dance Snake!' Sikander would applaud her. 'A very good song, Sudha. One day you must sing me the entire song.' 'Of course, of course,' she'd agree.

It was during this nicknaming period that they came up with the name, 'Kailasam'. Kailasam's real name was 'Sivagnanam'. His trousers, apparently, had been made by their family tailor. This tailor had made all his clothes since he was a child. Perhaps this man had never thought fit to change the pattern he had always used. At any rate, always when Kailasam leaned back or stretched his legs out when he sat down, his trousers would stick out at the crotch. Gunwant Kaur gave him the name 'Kailas Parbat', the Hindi version of 'Mount Kailasam'. She and Sudha shortened it to 'Kailasam'.

The nicknaming went on for several days. Then, suddenly, the craze left them just as speedily as it first came upon them. They discussed often whether the nicknames they gave the men were just a way of expressing their sexual feelings. The body, at that time, was beginning to be of huge importance to them. Its every cavity, every mound, every fold and every curve was a secret revealed. It was a time when the body took manifold forms and became a whole world. Kailasam was a small link in that world.

~

Kailasam was a little older than the rest of them. He had been a lecturer at a college for five years before he took up his research. He was not a lively man. He was not prone to sudden laughter. Somewhat stern features. Closely cropped hair. Well-shaven chin. Spectacles with a black frame. It was his opinion that the rest of them were immature. When they giggled at every little thing, he would reprimand them sometimes, saying, 'Be serious'. The reason why they hung about him was that they hankered after the ghee, the chutney powder, pickles, sweet and savoury snacks, the fruit which arrived for him in a constant flow from his family. They thought he was well aware of this.

One day Kailasam walked in while she was in the common room eating with relish one of the special bananas that had come for him from his home. There was no one else in the common room at the time. She could smell the string of jasmine flowers in the leaf-parcel he held in his hand.

He sat down next to her, suddenly, and gave her the

jasmine flowers. 'Why do you never wear flowers in your hair? Take these,' he said.

She was a little taken aback. 'What's this for?' she asked.

'You have lovely long hair. You haven't cut it all off like the others. It would look so beautiful if you wore the flowers.'

He was not one who said such things, usually. She was quite startled. She didn't refuse the flowers. When she tucked them into her hair casually, he said, 'Gently, gently. So that it doesn't hurt.'

He began to speak, as if reciting a lesson he had learnt by heart. 'Kamalam, I have fallen in love with you. I want to come close to you and touch you. I don't know anything about women. But I want to take you to myself entirely. I feel my body burning, night and day. Would you please marry me?'

'What's all this, Sivam?' she said, absolutely shocked now.

'Why, is it wrong of me to ask? Sometimes when you walk along with me, your hand falls on me. Sometimes your breast grazes against me, like fire. Even if its touch is as soft as a flower, it is fire, Kamalam.' Having blurted out all this, he made as if to kiss her.

'Sivam, please. This is awful. I don't like it,' she said, pushing him away.

He was trembling all over. His eyes had filled. 'Forgive me,' he said, and left the room.

He distanced himself from her after that. Before he left for England on fieldwork, he returned home. He came back, married. His wife, they were told, was a doctor. She too arrived, before his trip to London. There was no room in the university guest house at the time, and so when the warden asked her whether she would accommodate Kailasam's wife in her own large room at the end of the corridor, she could not refuse. It did strike her, however, that the couple could well have taken a room in a hotel, and stayed together.

Doctor Thenmozhi was a lively companion. She had an important position in a hospital and had the poise, dignity and smartness that went with it.

One evening, when Sudha and she were chatting together and lounging on her bed, Thenmozhi came in, unwound her sari, and put on her night-clothes.

'Doctor, where did you have dinner?' Sudha asked.

'At a restaurant in Connaught Place,' came the casual reply.

'At Nirula's?'

'Madras Café; meals. Today's special was sago *payasam*.' Thenmozhi sat down on her bed.

Sudha looked at her friend. She rose and made as if to leave.

Thenmozhi took hold of her hands and made her sit down again, saying, 'Stay awhile.' Then she asked, 'Have you two eaten?' She smiled at them both. And so the conversation began.

Thenmozhi was distantly related to Sivam. Plans for her marriage had been postponed for quite a while, as she had waited for a highly educated bridegroom who would respect her work. A family friend had told them about Sivam. And Sivam's father had carried out all the marriage negotiations. He had no mother; his aunt, his father's sister, was the one who brought him up. He had no siblings either. Thenmozhi very much approved of the fact that he was also a well-educated man. She saw him face-to-face only at their wedding; until then she was only acquainted with his photograph.

'What sort of man is Sivam?'

'You are the one married to him. Surely you know?' asked Sudha.

'No, Sudha. I have no idea who he is. He is certainly well behaved. He never loses his temper or anything like that. But he hasn't yet touched me. Even when we walk together, he never lays his hand on me. He never puts an arm around my shoulder to embrace me. I am saying all this to you two who are not even married yet, but please don't misunderstand me. He seems like a mere puppet without any passion, or strong feelings or desires of the body. He is a good man, of course. He hasn't spoken a single harsh word to me. I tried to convince him we should stay in a hotel, but he wouldn't listen. Now I'm putting you to such inconvenience, staying in your room . . . It seems to me that at some time in his life he became frozen inside. Who knows when he will melt . . .?'

Thenmozhi sat there, her head bowed, kneading her hands.

~

What are the secrets of a woman's body? What is the shape of her pubis? When you touch her pubic hair, will it be like silk, or coarse, like a blanket? An ancient poem likens it to a cobra rearing its head. What might Kamalam's pubis look like?

Is passion like an intoxicant? Subramania Bharati says, 'I am made dizzy', and adds, 'as if I had drunk a pot of mature toddy.' How can one come upon a pot of mature toddy in these parts? I talked the watchman into fetching me the local brew. But that intoxication was different; it shook up the body. What I feel is of a different nature. Once, when Kamalam bent over and reached across to pick something up, her breast touched me. I had a sudden sensation, as if I were floating gently. At the same time it was as if all the world's weight had fallen on my male member. On the one hand, a gathering heaviness; on the other, a weightlessness. Uncertainty. Dizziness. I gasped for breath.

Is this passion? I don't know the rules of desire.

∽

I am overwhelmed by passion.

∽

I want Kamalam to spin upon me like a ball of iron. I want her to press down on me. I want to flow over her like a ball made of flowers. Without hurting her, without crushing her.

∽

When I tighten my arms around her, I want her breasts to be squeezed against my chest. I want her nipples to stiffen and stand erect. I want to freeze forever inside her.

∽

In spite of so great a passion, her body never strikes me as a mere collection of limbs and organs. In my imagination, her body takes several forms: a river swirling as it flows;

a lake that is the refuge of many birds; the turbulent sea. I want to sink into her.

〜

One evening she was sitting in the common room, having slipped off her chappals. She sat on the sofa, with her knees drawn up, her face down on her knees, her eyes closed. She looked like a small hill, in her green sari. Her hair ran down her back like a black stream. Her feet were like newly open leaves.

〜

They describe women's features as edible things: eyes like grapes, apple cheeks, lips like ripe fruit. I think of myself as a rough piece of earth, full of stones, and thorny. I want Kamalam to plough me. I want her to turn me into arable land. Kamalam, though, is like marshy land. A mysterious region where you could be drawn within the mire at any step. I want to put my feet there, and daub myself with the wet earth. I want to sink into its bubbles. I want to make it fertile land.

〜

I want Kamalam to possess me.

〜

Will my member ever touch the entrance to her body? How will that touch be? Will it be like the cool thrill of the first drop of rain falling, after many thousands and many millions of years of waiting? Or will it be the sweet caress of fire?

〜

The telephone rang during the course of the morning. A woman's voice came on at the other end.

'Is Kamalam there, please?'

'This is Kamalam speaking.'

'I'm Dr Thenmozhi, Kamalam. Do you remember me?'

'Aren't you Sivam's wife?'

'So you still remember me? That's pretty good!'

'How come you're contacting me after all these years? And how did you find my telephone number?'

'I'll tell you when I come. I'm standing at the gate of your building, with my husband and children. May I come up now?'

'How can you ask? Yes, do come up, Thenmozhi.'

The doorbell rang. There were four of them. The person entering with Thenmozhi was not Sivam.

'Kamalam, this is my husband, Dr Kumarasamy. This is my son, Arun. He is a doctor, practising in the United States. This is my daughter, Arulmozhi. She too is a doctor. She wants to build a hospital of her own. At the moment, she works in Bangalore.'

They all sat down together and conversed generally, as they drank tea. After a while, Thenmozhi began to speak.

'Kamalam, Sivam and I separated within a year. There was no quarrel whatsoever. He was like a corpse, though. He himself said I should leave him. I met Kumarasamy in London, where I had gone for further studies. But I didn't cut myself off from Sivam totally. These children used to call him Periappa. After his father died, we were his only family. Kumarasamy and he became good friends. He became a professor locally, in Coimbatore. He lived alone like that, writing his research papers. He never married again. During the holidays he came to us; he'd stayed with us. Time went by in that way . . .'

It was as if what she said was a long prologue. It struck Kamalam that she spoke of Sivam in the past tense.

Thenmozhi continued, 'He had gone to Bangalore in order to make arrangements for building Arulmozhi's hospital. He went out for his walk in the morning, but never returned. It was winter weather. He could never endure the cold. As he was just leaving, Arulmozhi actually said to him, "Don't go, Periappa. It's very cold this morning." He didn't listen. He just wrapped his muffler round his head and went. Sometime later, his body was found in the Sankey Tank. We couldn't understand what happened, nor why. Perhaps, after he retired, he was yearning after something, we don't know. When we cleared his house of his belongings, this notebook came to light. On top, he had written all your addresses, ending with your latest one, and your phone number. I brought it away without opening it. Did he ever speak to you?'

'No, never. I still keep in touch with many of those friends. Sudha telephoned just last week. But I lost contact with him entirely.'

There was silence for a while. Then Thenmozhi took out a notebook from her bag. It had been placed inside a plastic folder. She held it out to Kamalam.

'You keep this now. He has written your name on top. Let him be at peace, somehow. Please don't take it amiss. We've given away all his books to the library. There wasn't much else. He had willed all his property to my children. He lived like a *sannyasi*, and now he's gone. What can we say? Because your name is written here . . .'

Kamalam accepted the notebook. She felt herself shaking as her fingers touched the plastic cover. She put it away on a table to one side.

Her visitors stayed a little longer, and then left.

The notebook lay on the table, within its plastic folder.

~

Gently she set aside the plastic folder. Inside, the hard cover was handmade. There were a few entries dated 1974, 1975. The rest of the notebook was empty.

~

A body at the bottom of the lake. A body which never gave anything away. A body which held all its secrets frozen within.

~

She sat down on a stool next to the refrigerator and leaned against it.

Kailasam, I never realized how much yearning you kept locked inside yourself. At that time, for me my body was a mystery, a riddle from which I had to free myself. I can only say I was just coping with my body. It was only later that I faced up to the hugeness of it. It was only gradually I learnt of its valleys, depths, scales, extensions, petals. I didn't dive into it and rise up fighting for breath, straightaway. It began very gently, and happened like the breaking of monsoons, accompanied by thunder. Like a song which begins softly, and reaches a peak with heightened rhythm.

When you approached me, I wasn't there. I was immersed in so many anxieties. About my research, about my future. It wasn't that I lacked any interest or curiosity about the male body, but it came and went like swiftly moving clouds. I didn't feel it with any depth.

You wrote about my pubis. At that time I wasn't aware of it myself. I never thought about the pubic hair upon it. Sometimes, during my periods, there was blood on it. Even when I washed it, it was done with indifference. People like me carried our bodies as if they were sinful burdens. The body was a cross one had to bear. That is what we were taught. The body could tip you into a deep and dangerous hole. You must stamp on the body, crush it, control it.

There was a young woman who worked in our house. She did the cooking. There were a couple of peons from my father's office who used to come and go, on errands, Raman Nair and Venkatappa. The other woman who worked for us, Narasamma complained to my mother that as she did the washing, Thangam kept exchanging glances with Raman Nair who waited under a tree. Soon after this, Amma reported that she too had caught them at it, 'red-handed'. After that, Raman Nair wasn't seen again. Thangam too was sacked. When I asked my mother why, she said that otherwise, a disaster could happen.

Sometime later, I chanced to meet Thangam at a music concert and asked her, 'Thangam what was the disaster that was going to happen because you looked at Raman Nair?'

'Who told you all this?' she asked.

'Amma.'

'No disaster happened. I just looked at him, that was all,' she said, smiling. She stroked my hair.

But the anxiety that my body possessed a capacity for bringing about disaster never left me. That truth about my body only began to reveal itself after I left home and went outside.

It was Narain Singh, a Trinidadian, who taught me to have a true vision of my body. He was an artist. When I was with him, my body shone like a natural landscape. Its mounds were transformed into mountains, its depths became valleys, its hidden parts were running streams. His body, too became other aspects of the same landscape. It too looped and curved and gave, like a creeper, like earth. It grew as dense as unploughed land. It tightened. It pulled like quicksands.

I thought it was love. It hurt when he started to go out with an American girl. Later, I became immersed in my other concerns. When I met him, two years later, he looked weary. He said he was very much alone. Some of us went to his house that day. When he approached me that night, I allowed him. The next morning I set off early, while the others were still asleep. Narain accompanied me to the bus station.

'When shall we meet again?' he asked.

'Never, Narain. Yesterday I saw you and felt sorry for you. That's why I agreed . . .' I said.

He was as shocked as if he had trodden on fire. 'You felt sorry for me?'

'What other reason could there be, Narain?'

'You've changed,' he said.

The bus arrived. I climbed in. I waved to him through the window. 'Life is a good teacher,' I said.

It became possible for me to give my body and take it back. It became possible to make it my own.

It was only with Dhananjayan that I learnt to accept my body with all its faults and its merits, neither over-rating nor undervaluing it. He allowed my body to fly. He returned it to my safe-keeping. He said I had taken his body to unknown regions, and established a path for its return. He said I redressed and balanced out the arrogance regarding the male body he had once held to. How wrong he had been to assume that the truth about a male body was its erect penis. When I pointed out the beauty of his penis as it lay prone, when we were not making love, he marvelled at the many meanings of the body.

It is now twenty-five years since we got married. I still don't understand about love, Kailasam. It is easy to understand passion. Love is not like that. The relationship between a man and a woman is extremely complicated. How much closeness there is in it, how much distance. How much that is hidden, how much that is open. How much violence, how much gentleness. How much rigidity, how much giving. How much tenderness, how much frenzy. There are times when you are angry enough to poison and kill the loved one. Then the anger ebbs away. It binds you in the closest of kinships. It comforts, like a nest. It burns. It cools.

When I consider my body as if it were a text, it isn't a stable text, Kailasam. It changes. Its appearances and meanings keep changing. My breasts have slackened and droop slightly. Green veins run along my thighs. And on my arms and legs too. My pubis is like a withered leaf. My pubic hair isn't thick and dense as before. Nor is it black. It has gone grey. It has lost its freshness, and looks dry.

Jayan's body too, shows many changes. His once-tightly-knit body is at times like clothes left soaking, ready to wash. When he comes out of his bath, his genitals, not yet dry, look curled up like a snail. The hair on his head is completely grey. Mine too. Even today I lean my breasts against his back and kiss his neck. He tells me he thrills then. When he strokes me, it is comforting. My hair stands on end.

So the body goes through many stages.

Why did you never contact me, Kailasam? You made Thenmozhi your friend, couldn't you have considered me as a friend, too? Had you asked me at another time in my life what you asked then, I don't know whether I would have agreed. But I don't think I would have shunned you.

Your body, which lay at the bottom of the lake, has now been cremated. Its ashes have been scattered on river waters. May that water, in which your ashes are dissolved, flow over a dry land. May grass grow upon the land, made fertile. May some cow or goat feast on that grass. May its udders fill with milk. May that milk sweeten some child's mouth.

Then may the river swell again, into a great flood that breaks its banks. May it flow over sand and stone and mud, bringing to life all that is parched. May it grow in richness. May a speck of those ashes become a seed, a plant, grow into a tree hung with fruit. May its branches look up to the skies.

~

The doorbell rang. When Kamalam woke from her reverie, the fridge had defrosted, and ran at her feet like a small rivulet flowing away from a great river.

Fish in a dwindling lake

As usual, all travellers arriving at the huge Kashmiri Gate bus station were plunged immediately into a state of confusion. Would her pre-booked ticket be valid? It wasn't possible for her to rush about here and there with her luggage, all by herself. She wanted desperately to go to the toilet, but couldn't go in, leaving her luggage abandoned outside. She stood there hesitating, with shoulder-bag, handbag and a bamboo basket containing rose cuttings. Finally, she left the basket outside and went in, carrying her bags. When she came out again, the bamboo basket was still there, safe, a small boy standing by, looking at it in surprise.

'Auntyji, is this yours?'

'Yes.'

'Shall I carry it for you?'

'It's not at all heavy; I can carry it myself.'

He stood there, watching her. She found an eight-anna coin from her purse and offered it to him. He refused to take it. She explained that she didn't like putting small children to work. He argued that if she gave him eight annas when he had not earned it, that would make him a beggar.

'Very well, you can put me on my bus,' she agreed.

Immediately, it felt as if she was being protected by a Black Cat patrol. As soon as she told him she was bound for a small town on the India-Nepal border, he started ahead of her swiftly, parting the crowds and almost swimming forward. In a short while they stood in front of the right bus. The person who had booked her ticket had informed her that the bus would be air-conditioned. As for this vehicle, it was covered in dust and looked like an actor whose make-up was in disarray.

The passengers, carrying their sacks and their huge trunks, were trying to load their luggage and fight their way into the bus, calling out at the top of their voices. She asked the conductor who was trying to cope with all these people, 'Is this the AC bus?'

'No, it's not air-conditioned, but it's the bus you want,' he replied, indifferently.

The small boy explained to her that this bus would stop in front of Anand Vihar in about an hour. There she must board the bus that would actually take her to her destination.

She asked whether the bus would stop conveniently for calls of nature. Certainly it would, the conductor told her. These would not be at proper toilets with running water. Instead, they usually stopped at deserted streets with an abundance of wild shrubs or tall trees nearby. Sometimes there wouldn't even be those to provide any privacy, only the darkness. On one occasion, on a dark night, the bus stopped at an unknown wasteland. She was the only woman to climb down. It was blindingly dark. There seemed to be some sort of building, locked up, nearby. She wandered about a bit, searching for a private place, and came to a wall where she squatted down. When she rose to her feet, a lorry hastened past, spitting its light in her direction. As she looked about her during that brief moment, her heart beat fast. She was standing next to a pedestal which carried a statue of Gandhi. There he was, his staff in his hand, one leg in front of the other, as if he were stepping forward. In her head, she asked him for forgiveness, 'Bapuji forgive me. You said: India would be truly independent when at last a woman, wearing all her ornaments, could go about freely in the middle of the night. You might have thought it important to mention ornaments specifically. We don't need a single ornament, Bapuji. We would be content if there were enough toilets for us, should we need to answer calls of nature, even at midnight. We'd be happy if there were toilets accessible in all the highways and chief places of independent India, so that women don't ever have to suffer, controlling themselves. Our bladders have grown weak from the strain of it. The urine, splashed freely by men, has made its mark on endless walls, starting from the temple wall; it's become a metaphor for freedom, indeed. The kings of long ago planted trees. They dug wells. They built inns and resting places. We don't know whether they established toilets. It seems to me this was our loss throughout the generations, Bapuji.' Her imagined conversation with Gandhi had continued like this, during that journey.

The small boy told her to climb in. He went in first and then called out to her. He had found her a window seat in the middle of the bus. He assured her there would be no problem with changing buses. The basket holding the rose cuttings slipped under her seat easily. The boy laid her shoulder-bag along the luggage rail above her. She held out a rupee note towards him. He ignored it and asked, 'Auntyji, don't you need some water?' She agreed she would, opened her handbag and gave him some money. He climbed out of the bus and ran. When he returned, he held in his hands a bottle of water and six bananas. Standing under her window, he held them out to her.

'Why the fruit?'

'You don't know, Auntyji, you'll get hungry. My village is right next to Mahendra Nagar, he told her, like one who had been sent on many journeys.

She pulled off two of the fruit from the bunch and gave it to him. He smiled as he accepted them. This time she handed him a five-rupee note. He hesitated a bit, but accepted that too.

The bus was filling up with foreign tourists, carrying heavy bags, and the usual passengers who were returning home. As the bus was making ready to start, the boy said goodbye to her. He called to her above the noises that the bus was making, 'Auntyji, in those parts, when the sky is clear you'll see snow-covered mountain peaks in the distance . . .' The bus began to move as the wind brought this information to her.

It struck her that snow-covered mountain peaks, revealed when the skies were clear, were a good goal for this journey.

~

Journeys had become the symbols of her life. Journeys with objectives, journeys without; meaningful journeys,

journeys made of necessity; journeys which were planned, but never happened; journeys which broke all decisions; journeys which had become rituals.

Her very birth was witness to her mother's final journey. She was the sixth child. After that, she became her elder sister's baby. When Didi married at the age of sixteen, and left her family on her *bidai* journey to her in-laws, she went with her, as part of her dowry. After that, her sister's husband, her Jijaji, became her new father. At intervals, she returned, to see her real father, elder sisters and elder brother. In spite of Jijaji's disapproval, her father insisted on arranging a marriage for her as soon as she finished her schooling, claiming that he was ready for his own last journey. Her life seemed to be ruled by other people's journeys, indeed. She set off on her own bidai journey with a man who had a slight frame and dim eyes. Later it came to light that he suffered from tuberculosis. As soon as he set foot on his final journey, before everyone could say she must break her bangles and remove her *kumkum*, her Jijaji arrived and took her away. There followed many journeys as she pursued her further education. Journeys to do with her profession, first as a lecturer in Delhi, then as she rose to become a professor. Journeys undertaken after Didi died, to look after her children and to educate them. Journeys with Didi's youngest son, who had to have electric shock treatment for his psychiatric problems. Journeys with Jijaji when he had cancer, for radiotherapy. Journeys within the country and journeys abroad. A life threaded together by journeys.

After she retired from work, Didi's sons and daughters, who were now United States citizens, had demanded affectionately that she go and live with them in California,

New York, Washington and Boston. She had made up her mind to do so. And now, all of a sudden, she was bound on this journey. Entirely by accident.

The arguments and counterarguments between her and those Indians who no longer lived in India, had lasted for a whole year.

'So what is so wonderful in India, Mausi, apart from dust and noise and crowds? Why don't you come and see what it's like here?'

'You won't have to roast in the sun nor be drenched in the rain. There will be a whole world within your home.'

'You won't have to rush about for anything here. There will be no worries at all for you. This is a world which works at the touch of a button, without any problems.'

'You've been here as a postgraduate student, haven't you? You know very well what it's like.'

She had indeed lived in that world for a while. It was a world with many choices. Even when she tried to buy a sandwich, she had faced a number of choices. White bread or wholemeal? What sort of butter? With fat or without? Vegetarian or otherwise? What sort of salad or meat? Should they add gherkins or other relishes, or not? Grilled sandwich, or plain? Did she want cheese or not? After she had answered all these questions, there was the final one. Would she eat her sandwich in the premises or take it away?

Here life didn't have so many choices. Nor many buttons to press. It was only after she arrived at Delhi that she even came across a doorbell.

At home, in the village, their front door was always open. Women carrying their water pots home would often set them down and rest in their front veranda. They'd pack their mouths with betel leaves and call out to Didi for a chat. Drivers of horse carts would help themselves to water from the big earthenware pot there, and quench their thirst. One of them was a great singer of folk ballads. Once he had drunk some water, he'd summon all the children in their family and sing to them in his resounding voice. Once, a patron of arts invited him and his group to Paris. He went there, wore his colourful turban, raised his voice and sang loudly, and then came back. After that, he drove his horses as usual. If asked, 'What was Paris like?', he answered casually, 'Not bad. Rather big.' There was no change in his lifestyle, apart from a picture of the Eiffel Tower in his cart.

Sometimes the cow, Kalavati, which had gone grazing, would come and stand at their front veranda. 'Mma,' it would call out to Didi. It had once eaten a few pages out of Munna's homework book. Jijaji scolded the child for leaving her notebook there. Now, many years later, in New York, Munna's son did his homework on the computer. How would a cow turn up there? Nowadays, the milk, yielded by nameless cows, arrived pasteurized, anyway.

Stories all of them: the bridegroom arriving on an elephant; the camels padding across the desert sands; the annual camel races; the children dressed as brides and grooms, with *laddoos* or *jalebis* in their hands during Akkha Teej; peacocks spreading their dark green and blue feathers as they flew to the low-lying branches of the trees and sat there; comfortingly warm *razzais* made of old saris sewn together; saris knotted and dyed dark blue and indigo and red, the colours spreading as soon as the knots were undone and the saris shaken out. Stories, all of them, from beginning to end. Stories she told their children, and the children of friends and relatives. And the children assumed that they were tales of magic, like Harry Potter stories. Many of the heroes and heroines of those stories were no longer alive. But some of them were. The horse-cart driver still sang in the evenings, after his drink of toddy. The horse was no longer there, nor the cart. He told his grandchildren the tale of his journey to Paris. They were special magic tales to them. Some months ago, walking along a path dense with trees and bushes, she stumbled over a peacock which lay dead, obstructing her path, its feathers shorn. Was it magic or real? It was all magic; it was all true.

In this bus which tore through the night, sitting with her bamboo basket of rose cuttings together with unknown individuals, sacks, trunks, foreign bags, cloth bundles, cloth bags full of clothes, on this sudden and accidental journey, she didn't know what was real, what was magic.

～

A couple of days after she decided to live abroad permanently, she received a letter from Bimla Devi. It had been written on paper headed with the name and address of the Lok Seva Sangh which she ran. The letters were printed in saffron, on a white background. Bimla had written in her usual dark blue ink. She asked her please to visit, and to bring some cuttings from a rose nursery in Delhi when she came; she, Bimla, would be looking forward to her arrival. She had been a little surprised by the letter. It was now some years since she had lost contact with Bimla Devi. She had withdrawn herself after everyone began calling Bimla Devi 'Mataji' and 'Sadhviji'. Bimla had not shown any disapproval when people addressed her like this. Neither did she ask that she should be addressed thus.

Bimla Devi and she were classmates when they were at university. Later, for some time, Bimla taught history in the same college where she was employed. She was the first, in a family of agricultural labourers, to seek out higher education. Mid-brown skin. Long hair, combed flat. Eyes which darted about everywhere, like fish swimming around in a glass bowl. A dazzling smile. Strong arms and legs. A strong body, not afraid of toil. Because the two of them found it difficult to speak English fluently, they became room-mates and friends. During her holidays, with Jijaji's permission, she went to stay with Bimla Devi's family. Although, by that time, they owned sufficient land, they worked on it themselves. She had never seen Bimla's father in laundered clothes. In her memory his legs were always mud stained, his face sweaty. Bimla and her mother worked in the fields and at home untiringly. They were constantly at work, weeding, carrying loads, cleaning out the cowshed, looking after their poultry, cooking meals. Besides, she would go to graze the goats, along with her brothers. The background music in that household was the jingling of Bimla's mother's green glass bangles.

She was not one who shirked hard work, either. Didi, too, was one who laboured hard and tirelessly. But there were servants in their house as well. When she visited Bimla's family, she was eager to join in with the others in their daily chores. She failed abysmally at the task of grazing the goats, however. She admitted to Bimla and her siblings, that it was not an easy task to gather the herd together, nor to separate it into smaller groups. They tended to laugh at her. It seemed to her that even the goats joined in with that laughter. Only one small black kid clung to her side and comforted her.

After she started visiting Bimla's family regularly, she too picked up the habit of chewing tobacco. Bimla's mother always had a wad of tobacco leaves tucked inside her mouth. Bimla often said to her mother, 'Maji, please don't go any further than the tobacco. Don't go and get her used to toddy as well. She shares a room with me in the college . . .' When Bimla's father came home in the evenings, tired out, he had a drink of toddy. He sat in the backyard, next to the cowshed, and drank his toddy. Her mother, too. Sometimes, her brothers joined them, squatting down and drinking. They usually had their drink away from the house, at the toddy shop. Only occasionally did they gather together in the backyard, squatting together. They avoided drinking inside the house, or in front of Bimla. Beyond the cowshed, there was a rose garden covering an acre of land. The toddy drinking took place there, when she and Bimla went out on their evening walks. When they returned they would just glimpse their backs, turned away.

It struck her, sometimes, that the rest of the family treated Bimla with a special respect. The others in the village—including those who were well off, and belonging to higher castes—appeared to speak to her with deference. When she asked Bimla about it, Bimla laughed it off. She spoke to everyone with ease, touching them. At college, once, when the daughter of a lowly employee was taken into hospital after a suicide attempt, Bimla spoke to the father, putting her hand on his shoulder to comfort him.

He broke down then, and began to weep. He held her hand and wept aloud. Sometimes, the college lecturers spoke to Bimla about personal matters. Bimla never gave anyone any advice. She never preached any dogmas. She never attended any rituals or pujas in anyone's homes. Yet she seemed to attract everyone in some way which was other than materialistic or mundane. She gave out a sense of comfort. Once their college mates had joined together to make up a farce about Bimla's special nature, which they acted out at one of their evening celebrations. Bimla just laughed at that too.

Once she was sitting with Bimla's mother, cleaning a chicken and cutting it up. When she thought about it later, that short conversation, and the background to it, returned to her mind like a scene in a play. Preparations for their mid-day meal were going on in the kitchen. The wheat flour had been kneaded and set aside. Dal was bubbling on the firewood hearth. Sliced onion, potato and other vegetables. The chicken pieces had been marinated in curds. A smell of mingled onion, garlic and ginger. Rays of light fell through the small window of the kitchen with its low, thatched roof. The cowshed could be seen through the window, outside. Bimla was cleaning it out. That was when she asked her the question, 'Maji, when will Bimla get married?'

'Bimla? We'll see,' said her mother, as if it were not a matter of concern.

She thought perhaps that Bimla's mother hadn't liked her asking this question. But in a while the answer came, 'If ever Bimla wants a family or a marriage, then we'll arrange it.'

'Why, doesn't she want to get married?'

'It doesn't seem so. Let's see what Swamiji Maharaj will say.'

The conversation came to an end as the marinated chicken pieces dropped with a sizzling noise into the earthenware pot with its hot oil seasoned with cinnamon, clove and fennel seeds.

~

They took Swamiji Maharaj by his hand and led him to a seat in the front of the house. He was blind, and bare-bodied, except for the small piece of cloth wound about his waist.

'Whose house is this, tell me.'

'It belongs to Madangopal Misraji. He has a hundred acres of land.'

'The land will be the land's. How can it be his?' He laughed aloud.

They brought him a small water-pot full of water. 'Please talk to us, Swamiji Maharaj.'

'It was terribly hot. A fiery heat that burnt the body. Later, the rain fell. Not a rain with blustering winds, but a rain that fell in straight strands. A rain like a shower of flowers. That was when it came and clung to my legs. I lifted it up. A puppy. It licked my face. This Govind told me it was black and white. It was he who named it Kalu. However many miles I walked, it would follow me. At nights it would sleep, rolled up against my feet. People began to call me "The Dog Maharaj". Now there's no dog. Just the Maharaj.' He laughed again.

'Please, Swamiji Maharaj, say something that will be useful to us in our lives.'

'Something useful?'

'Yes, perhaps something from the Bhagavad Gita . . .'

'The Bhagavad Gita? What do I know of the Bhagavad Gita? I am a wanderer, a constant traveller, a vagabond and gadabout. I drink water anywhere, eat everywhere, sleep and wake up wherever I please. I said I was thirsty; this Govind brought me here.'

'In that case, why don't you come to my house too,' a shrill voice piped up.

Swamiji Maharaj turned in the direction from where the voice came. So did the others. A five-year-old girl with her satchel of books, leaning against a pillar, her hand at her waist. A girl who should not have stepped into houses belonging to people such as Misraji.

Swamiji Maharaj smiled. 'O, you are here, are you, little girl? Come here and take my hand.'

She came running up and took his hand. She slung her satchel across her shoulder. Before anyone could stop him, the blind man followed as she pulled him along.

~

They were stunned when they saw him. Where should they ask him to sit? What should they give him to eat? A portion of the cattle shed in Bimla's house was cleaned and tidied. He sat down there.

'Maharaj, what should we give you to eat? We have cooked beef in this house today.'

'Beef, is it? You eat and enjoy. Have you made rotis?'

'Yes.'

'A couple of rotis and a squashed onion will be enough for me.' An onion was squashed by hand, seasoned with salt and pepper, and laid on top of hot rotis. They gave him this. He ate with relish, and slept soundly in the cattle shed. He stayed with them for fifteen or twenty days.

~

The people of those parts wanted a temple. Swamiji Maharaj was not interested in that. He arranged for them to gain ownership of the fallow land lying beyond the cattle shed, which lay unused. He went here and there and brought them the rose cuttings. He instructed them to plant the roses. Roses came up in the land which had been thought unusable. A co-operative farm for rose cultivation began to take shape, gradually expanding into other businesses such as manufacturing attar and making rose garlands and bouquets for shrines and dargahs. A small hut was raised for him, right next to the rose garden.

Those who once called him 'Dog Maharaj' now began to call him 'Rose Maharaj' instead. He still walked on his journeys.

~

These were all supplementary stories told about Swamiji Maharaj. Stories everyone told, with embellishments, or otherwise. He had said he knew neither magic nor magical spells. For those who came to him, refusing to believe this, he dispensed neither sacred ash nor *kumkum*. He could walk. For the sake of the rose garden. For the sake of educating the poor. A small piece of cloth around his waist. A face obscured by a white beard. Blind eyes. A loud laugh.

~

Bimla's mother had told her in detail about the event that took place a couple of days after he moved in with them. It was dusk: that time of day when all the cows were returning home. The air was full of the call of birds flying home to their nests. At this time, people would gather to see Swamiji, in the hut they had put up for him. That day too, some people were sitting in front of him. As soon as Bimla came running up with her satchel of books and stood by the front door, he was aware of her arrival. He spread his hands towards her and said, 'Come'. She set down her satchel and ran up to him. He stroked her hair and kissed her forehead. Then he leaned down and spoke softly into her ear. Just one second. Her expression registered shock and surprise. Then, gradually, her face began to blossom like a flower. As soon as he moved his head away from her ear, five-year-old Bimla hugged him and kissed his white-bearded face. Swamiji Maharaj gathered her tightly to his heart.

~

When she asked Bimla about that incident once, she didn't get an answer immediately. Some of them used to sleep on the terrace, in the heat of the summer. There were charpoys there, for that purpose. That evening they both lay on their beds there, gazing up at the sky. When she asked her question, Bimla continued to look at the sky intently, as if her gaze were piercing through the stars. Then she said softly, 'I'm not sure I can explain it clearly . . .'

'Why? Can't dimwits like me understand, or what?'

She laughed. 'No, it isn't that', she said in a low voice. 'But language has its limits, doesn't it?'

There was silence for a while.

'Kumud, what he spoke in my ear can't be contained in words. First it was like the buzzing of a bee. Then the rustling of running water. After that, the sensation of a great flood on which I floated like a cork, weightlessly. Then the sensation of hurtling back and forth on a swing, and then gradually, very gradually coming to a stop and climbing off. The way you feel after those games we play, holding hands and whirling round. A feeling of unbounded, unlimited love flowing within me and stroking me, like the milk pouring down in consecration over the temple images . . .'

She fell asleep as Bimla went on with her description.

~

She, too, met Swamiji Maharaj on one occasion. She had no particular desire to meet him. In fact she shunned all so-called swamijis. When Roop Kanwar lay beside the corpse of her husband and set fire to herself, many of her college lecturers had taken out a procession to protest against the superstitious belief in sati. Without exception, all the swamijis who were interviewed on television had declared, 'Women who go out on these processions are immoral. They have relations with more than one man.' They were all there, complete with their matted locks, their sacred ash and sandalwood paste, bald heads and religious forehead-marks. Even though a very few, such as Swamiji Maharaj had supported them, on the whole she avoided all religious sages.

Once Didi had insisted she accompany her to see the head of a religious mutt from the south of India. The people at the door had asked them a hundred questions about their caste and sub-caste, and found out that Kumud was a widow. Immediately they said, 'We can't give you permission to go in; if he sees widows he will have to fast.' She had never before seen Didi so furious. 'It would be a good thing if he were to look at her and then fast. We're leaving. Tell him to eat . . .' she had said, and gone home. Later she had fought with Didi, attacking her for believing in swamijis.

When Didi was at the point of death, she had asked, hesitantly, 'Please will you ask Bimla to come.' Bimla did come. She was still teaching at the college in those days. Didi's eyes filled as soon as she saw her. 'Bimla, Beti, I want to die in my sleep,' she said. Her face was twisted in an unbearable pain. Bimla began to stroke her forehead. In a while Didi had fallen asleep. Bimla never left her side. At about half past four the next morning, Didi's breath fell away, gradually. All the wrinkles on her face had disappeared, as if they had been smoothed out. At once Bimla had her bath and prepared to leave. She said she was going to Rishikesh with Swamiji Maharaj.

It was ten or fifteen years after this that she herself met Swamiji Maharaj. Didi's youngest daughter had finished her studies in the United States, and had decided to marry an American. Her fiancé's family believed that India was a country full of snake-charmers, elephants and tigers. They imagined it to be a country where the food was hot and spicy, the women dark and voluptuous, wearing brightly-coloured clothes; the country of the *Kamasutra* and of the great sages, but also a country riddled with poverty, disease and beggars; a land that could delight in many different ways. The bridegroom wanted to arrive in procession, riding on an elephant, and did so, amidst delighted cries of 'Ohs' and 'Ahs'. As she stood watching the procession, a sob rose in her throat, like a sudden stroke of paralysis. Before she could understand it, more sobs followed. Her eyes filled. Jijaji who was doing an errand nearby, noticed her and came up. 'Well, Kumud, your girl has grown up, hasn't she? Hereafter she too will set up a home, a family . . .'

She nodded, quietly.

He looked at her again, and said, 'What is it, Kumud, what has happened?'

Like a flash of lightning, the words which had been formulated at some time, somewhere, came out of her, shocking her. 'Jijaji, you could have arranged another marriage for me, couldn't you? Why didn't you do it?'

Jijaji was utterly shaken. She was forty years old at the time. 'You . . . you . . .' he stuttered in confusion. He put his arm around her shoulder and hugged her. Her eyes were blinded with tears, preventing her from seeing the bridegroom arrive in elephant procession.

During the course of a conversation, later on, she had told Bimla how, for that instant, her own words had taken her by surprise.

The next time Swamiji Maharaj was in town, Bimla insisted that Kumud accompany her to the place where he was staying. During those many years, Swamiji had set up Lok Seva Sanghs in several places. Adjacent to each ashram, but outside it, there was a rose garden, and a small hutment for him to stay. He had come to stay in Delhi, with a social worker. Kumud had gone with Bimla, at last, after she invited her several times. A number of people had gathered there to see the Swamiji. A couple of men who had failed in their Civil Service exams had turned up, saying they wished to become *sannyasi*s.

'Then why don't you do it?'

'Training . . .' The word was dragged out.

'Training? Can you stand hunger? Can you endure disrespect? Are you able to sleep in a space of two square yards? If you can, you are certainly a sannyasi.'

'Initiation . . .'

'If a hand is placed on your head, that is an initiation. Do it yourself.'

They had come prepared to renounce the whole world, and now stood aside, a little disappointed.

A woman, a singer, was eager to sing to him. He asked her to do so. The Mira bhajan that the woman sang seemed to echo her own state of mind at the time. She felt as if pushed down to the lowest possible state in life.

The woman sang, '*Hey Govind, Hey Gopala, ab tho jivan haari*', 'I have given away my life now'.

When she sang this, Kumud felt herself choking. Her throat ached as if a thorn were stuck there. She felt ashamed. That this should happen at a place where she knew no one other than Bimla.

Swamiji looked in the direction from where the voice came and said, 'It was that Mira alone who was able to lose her life. Beat it as you will, it always bounces back, like a ball that returns to the hand. It is not so easy to give away your life.'

She went and made her obeisance to him and left.

People like him would never understand. It wasn't spirituality that she needed at that time. A husband with a robust body at the right age. One or two babies who grew and hung heavy in the womb, and in due time pushed, shoved and tore their way past the birth canal, covered in blood. Or even three or four babies. Breasts running with milk. It was all part of the body. The body was the only truth she knew. It was the body alone that was left, even as she went beyond the body. She needed an oar to begin that crossing. She needed a boat and a boatman. Her body was the river. It was itself the shore. It was the hunter and the hunted; the path and the goal.

~

After that came the rise in her career at college. Her worries about Jijaji's health and of her care of him. So the years went past. A distance grew between Bimla and herself. Bimla came when Jijaji died. She was the same old playful Bimla. All the same, as she entered the house it seemed to Kumud that a flame of fire had walked in. Bimla wore a saffron shawl draped over her customary pale-coloured handloom cotton sari. Later Kumud thought it had been the sorrow of that moment and her eyes swollen with tears that had exaggerated her vision of Bimla.

Later still, many people asked her, 'Do you know Mataji Bimla Devi?', 'Is Sadhvi Bimla Devi a close friend of yours?', 'Is it true she embraces everyone she meets?'

Gradually, she lost contact with Bimla, after that. Occasionally she received a postcard from her, with brief news such as which town Bimla was visiting, and when. And now, this letter. Kumud didn't get a place on the train. Neither was there a direct train which would take her to her destination. This novel bus journey was the result.

~

The rains had failed that year. Everywhere along the way, she saw a withered green. Everywhere, a land that was thirsty. When she reached her destination, she was told she must travel some distance by rickshaw in order to reach the small town where she was headed. Asking the way at small shops scattered here and there, she finally reached the place where the Lok Seva Sangh was located. She went up to a man who stood at the doorway, and said she was Bimla Devi's friend. Immediately she was shown into a small reception room and asked to sit down.

In a little while, she heard Bimla calling her by name, 'Kumud'. And then she was there in person. She had grown very thin. At once Kumud rose to her feet, went up to her, took her by the hand and embraced her. 'How did you know it was I? You must have so many people coming to see you.'

'But he told me it was my friend. And aren't you my only friend,' she said. She smiled.

'Here are the rose cuttings you wanted. I bought them from the same rose nursery that you mentioned. But this bus journey has broken my back, I tell you. There were potholes and dips all along the bus route. We were well and truly flung about.'

'Come. Come and have a hot bath. I've kept some really good tobacco just for you. We'll talk later.'

As they came out of the room Bimla said to the man they encountered, 'Sukhbir, your rose cuttings have arrived. Look, she's brought them.'

'Oh, very good,' he said, walking on.

~

Her health had been failing for some months, she said. It seemed she had begun to get better only recently, and very gradually. She hadn't recovered fully as yet. A common friend of theirs, Urmila, had told her about Kumud's intention to leave the country for ever and live abroad. She spoke as she lay on her bed. She said her spine hurt. From time to time, her face was bathed in sweat. Even as Kumud wiped Bimla's face with a towel tenderly, hot words came out of her mouth. As if she were continuing with an argument which started somewhere, at some time, she asked, 'Bimla, in the end it is this pain that is the truth. Isn't that so?'

'It too is the truth.'

'You always denied the body. Now, see, all that is left is the body.'

'Who denied the body?'

'You. You did. I lost mine because of the decisions made by all kinds of others. But the body alone is certain. The truth. You denied this truth. The body's urine, shit, blood; its desires, hunger and thirst are all truths.'

'It isn't quite like that, Kumud,' Bimla said gently. 'The body has several aspects to it. Its appearance, its everyday functions may seem to be common experience, but the truth of each individual body will be different from anyone else's. The body is indeed an anchorage. But each body casts anchor in a different sea. Everything external—trees and plants, creepers, forests, beasts--all of it is the body. Only the body. Without the body, there is nothing. Everything is through the body. You can keep on stretching the boundaries and limits of the body. It will accept everything, contain everything. It will be able to mingle with everything.'

Once more her face was bathed in sweat. Kumud wiped it away.

~

She explained why she had invited Kumud to come there.

She arrived at this mountain village some years ago, entirely by chance, she said. A conference on spirituality was to be held at a small town nearby, to which several women had been invited. People from different groups were expected to participate: a great number, including Catholic nuns, Sufis, Jains, Parsis, Sikhs, people like Bimla, people who insisted on harmony amongst religions, activists. Bimla was travelling with some nuns, in two or three compartments. At about half past eight, after they had finished dinner together, a young nun, left for her own compartment. It was only a couple of hours later that they realized she had never got there. Terrified, they looked everywhere for her, and found her at last, fallen down in the bathroom. She had been raped. All over her body were scratched with a razor-blade, the syllables 'Om', 'Om'. They had written their religion on her body. It lay there, a symbol of the violence that religions are capable of. The conference took place against the backdrop of this tragedy.

They concluded that the only weapons they had against such madness were education and good health. To create healthy bodies and healthy minds. Many among them were skilled in these two fields. On their way back, she stopped at this village for a couple of days. She wanted to start a school here. To build a hospital. Swamiji Maharaj was at the last stage of his life, at that time. He told her she had made an excellent decision.

'So who is likely to come to this school then? There are only about fifty houses in this village, I think.'

'There are several villages hereabouts. There might even be children coming across the border.'

'Very well. You summoned me here because of your dream school. What about your hospital?'

'Why, there's Sukhbir. He's a doctor.'

'Really? And there was I, thinking he was the gardener.'
Bimla laughed.

'Look here, Bimla. Why don't you travel around to cities here and there, giving your sermons? Go abroad. Travel the world over and talk about your thoughts and the lifestyle you believe in. What is there for you in this place? Only ignorance and corruption, and a life lacking enough money to do what needs to be done. Why should you be confined to India? And that too in this village which doesn't even appear on a map of India.'

'Kumud, did you see the book Ira Pande wrote about her mother, Shivani? It describes how Shivani went to visit her elder sister, who was failing in health. Shivani asked her, you have a house in a pleasant setting in the hills, why can't you go and live there instead of staying in this place. The answer her sister gave her is the same answer I should give you.'

'And what was that?'

'You read it yourself. Or ask Sukhbir; he'll tell you.'
Bimla closed her eyes.

When the lake dwindles, the birds fly away,
seeking their nests elsewhere.
Yé Rahim! Fish lacking wings,
where can they go?

A poem by Abdul Rahim Khan-e-Khana, who lived in Akbar's time.

'In that case, Sukhbir, they are fish to be pitied. Fish that will die when the lake dwindles away.'

'No, not so. Fish that believe that the rains will come. Fish that are not afraid to die. Fish that wait for the lake to fill again. Fish that have become one with the lake . . .'

~

Dreams. Mere dreams. They were trying to entangle her in those dreams. But she was a free bird. The four people she had raised were all living abroad. She had a room in each of their homes. If she grew tired of one home, she would be welcome in another. She need not be imprisoned in any one of them. Bimla and Sukhbir may have very good reasons for their plans here. Sukhbir had studied medicine at a foreign university, and had worked in a big hospital in India on his return. One evening, when he was driving his car very fast, he crashed into a family, and all of them died instantaneously: husband, wife and two children. One of the children was a baby in arms. Shocked, he stopped the car and rushed towards them. The woman, holding the baby to herself, called out with her dying breath, 'Ei, you sinner, you destroyed my entire family.' The verdict at the court proved favourable to Sukhbir. But those eyes filled with panic at the moment of death, chased after him. 'Ei, you sinner, you sinner . . .'

He took refuge with Swamiji Maharaj. During the first four years, he planted all of the Lok Seva Sangh rose nurseries, and cared for them. Four crore roses for four lives. Four Years. Then he established hospitals at all branches of the ashram, and appointed appropriate staff. He said that even now, he saw those eyes on some nights, accusing him. He was past sixty now. When she asked why he had not gone away and worked elsewhere, he said that no country had a border that would prevent those eyes from following him. They were eyes written upon his body, he said. He never stopped from laying out rose gardens.

But Kumud was not held fast by anything. There was nothing that pulled her to itself.

Sunk in thought, she had walked some distance. Nothing was cooling to the eye. The mountains were at a great distance. During her bus journey, she had glimpsed, now and then, spotted deer, and peacocks with their tails outspread, even though there was no sign of rain. Here there was nothing at all.

A barbed-wire fence stopped her from going any further. Beyond it, a pond. A little girl stood at its further shore. Bare-bodied, except for a small skirt about her waist. A stick in her hand. She too was like that as a little girl. Didi could not cope with all the children. Kumud would run off towards the fields, a stick or a doll held in her hand. She'd sit under the shade of a tree and think of the photograph of her mother which hung in their home. What had her mother been like? Was she as loving as Didi? But Didi never had any time. Everything was done in a hurry. Bathtime was a rush. Making the rotis was a rush. Serving the food was a rush. She had to go to school, didn't she? When Didi returned home in the evening, there were more constraints. It wasn't possible for her to sit on Didi's lap. But her mother must have had lots of time. Her mother would have laid her on her lap.

Stroked her hair. Hummed a song to her in a low voice. At the thought, tears would gather in her eyes.

Grasping the barbed wire in her hands, she wept. The tears came, in great sobs. In an unfamiliar town, in this unknown place, these tears in the presence of a barbed-wire fence. The pond was witness; the little girl the spectator. She felt someone touch her hand. The little girl was standing next to her, on the other side of the fence. Her hair had been plaited in five sections. The plaits stood out, like sticks.

'Mausiji, why are you crying?'

'Some dust in my eyes. How did you get here?'

'The pond isn't deep. I waded across.'

'Don't you have school?'

'Our house doesn't have a door.'

'I asked why you haven't gone to school.'

'That's what I'm telling you. Our house doesn't have a door.'

'Where's your house, then?'

'Over there. Quite far off. Now Mataji is going to build a school for us. I can come and study there in the evenings. Babuji and Maji will have come home by then, won't they?'

'So who's at home now, in your house?'

'Dada's there. Otherwise the dogs will come and upturn all the food. We don't have a door to our house, you see.'

A girl who couldn't go to school, who safeguarded a house without doors from prowling dogs.

'What's your name?'

'Chunari.'

'Would you like to go to school?'

'I want a notebook, pencil and everything.'

'And then?'

'Mausiji, I know lots of stories. I want to tell them all to the teacher. Mataji promised us. She'll build a school.'

She crawled underneath the fence and came beside her. 'Mausiji, do you know this? You can walk all the way to Nanda Devi from here.'

'Is that so?'

'Yes, and after that, if you walk and walk and walk a long, long way, you'll see the Panchuli Mountain range. There are five mountains in all. The five Pandavas made a hearth out of all five mountains and cooked their food.'

'When was this?'

'Before they went up to heaven.'

'Who told you all this?'

'I just know it by myself.'

'Very good.'

A cool breeze blew. A couple of raindrops splashed on Chunari's cheek. Then they fell on her head too. It began to drizzle.

'Rain, rain,' sang out Chunari. She too, wanted to sing aloud.

Chunari had been laughing, chuckling and snorting. Suddenly she stopped. 'I must go,' she said. 'Dada will scold me.'

She was just about to step forward and crawl under the fence, but turned round and came back. 'Mausiji, please don't cry.'

'No, I won't. I won't cry.'

'When Mataji builds her school, you too will get a pencil and notebook and everything. You mustn't cry.'

'I won't.'

She crawled beneath the fence, and in an instant had crossed the pond and reached the other side, scattering water and drenching her skirt. Running, she disappeared.

Kumud stood there until she was drenched to the skin. The rain water seeped through her, with the chill wind. She felt as if she had been scoured clean. The barbed-wire fence she held, the withered trees accepting the rain, the pond which lay there like a thirsty mouth opening, Chunari with her little skirt, the small boy who had bought her bananas in that crowd-tossed bus station, anticipating her hunger, the snow-covered mountain peaks he said you could see when the skies cleared—everything entered her body and came out again, spreading, spreading everywhere and taking universal form. Her body diminished into a dot—a single dot among the several that were all strung together.

~

It was evening. Bimla Devi sat in an easy chair by the window, her eyes shut. The pale pink light of dusk fell on her face. Her spine must have ached. She grimaced very slightly, now and then. She looked as if she had lived through many centuries. As if she was beyond age. As if she had achieved eternal life.

'Bimla,' she called, gently.

She opened her eyes and smiled.

Kumud went and sat next to her. 'Does it hurt a lot?' she asked.

'Rather a lot.'

'Bimla, the rains have come,' she said.

'Yes. We have been waiting anxiously.'

'Bimla, we can put up fences behind the ashram, and make a thatched shed. It will house the first five classes. We need to order from Bareilly or some other town, blackboards, chalk, notebooks, pencil, textbooks and everything. Bimla, we must have book bags, mustn't we? And then, Bimla, would it be possible to give the children a cup of hot milk every day?' Her voice seemed to echo. Bimla was peacefully asleep, holding on to Kumud's hands. She was breathing evenly.

Journey 8

For some reason, the Hamsadvani ragam echoed through her head all the time, just before she went to see him. She didn't know music. But she did know that at the beginning of every musical performance, the invocation to Ganesha was set to the Hamsadvani ragam. A ragam that brought a sudden joy. It had the ability to draw you out, like a dying lamp that glows again, when its wick is drawn out. A ragam which starts something going in your head. A ragam which seemed to go up a creeper on the ascending scale of *sa-ri-ga-pa-ni-sa,* pluck the flower at the very top, and then climb down again on the descending scale of *sa-ni-pa-ga-ri-sa,* the flower in its hand.

In the story she had selected for a half-hour film, too, a relationship should be brought alive suddenly. An instant's spark bringing about a closeness. She had decided to ask Gopi Narayanan to compose the background music for the film. When she approached him though, he admitted with some shame but quite a lot of pride all the same, that he was completely tied up with composing jingles for films advertising toothpaste. As well as this, he was making up catchy tunes to match the arousal of women in films advertising men's underpants. He had won the last year's award for the best advertising jingle, apparently. His *vina* lay safely, in a corner of his house.

He melted a little, when he saw the look of disappointment in her face. He mentioned the name of a musical genius who had composed music since the earliest years of the advertising world; of whom it was said that at one time, there wasn't a single advertising film whose music was not of his composition. All the contemporary musicians of worth had trained under him. Including Gopi Narayanan himself. He had been trained in both Carnatic and Hindustani classical music traditions. He was an expert at Western music as well. Nowadays, though, he wasn't so busy. He had reached the age of seventy-five. Gopi Narayanan assured her that he was the only hope for people such as she, who tried to make films with little money to hand; only their dreams and imagination. He was a Tamil, this man, named Balsub. When she asked him what sort of Tamil name that was, he said it was short for Balasubramaniam. The consequence of having lived in Mumbai for fifty years. He gave her Balsub's telephone number. Before she left, he gave her a couple of hints: he said this Balsub was a very simple fellow, and somewhat strange. When she asked in what way, he answered that he kept a monkey as a pet. She had seen enough strange sights such as sparrows, parrots, dogs as big as calves and white rats being kept as pets in the narrow tenement houses in Mumbai. Surely, she wasn't going to be startled by a monkey.

The telephone number was for the Marine Drive area. Quite a distance from Mira Road. When she spoke to him on the telephone, he sounded very hesitant. He agreed to meet her only upon her insistence. All along that journey, the Hamsadvani ragam played in her head. In her hand she held a neat printout of the story in a plastic folder. That was how the journey went; her Hamsadvani journey.

The street was at a curve next to Marine Drive. All the buildings there were old apartment blocks. Where else would someone who was famous in the advertising world live? When she gave his name to the caretaker of the apartment block, he signalled that she should go towards the back of the building. Wondering whether there could be a mansion at the back of the building, she walked on, and found only garages with doors that rolled down, all of them closed. Right in the corner, there was one garage which remained open. Rubbish overflowed from the big plastic drums which the municipality had not yet cleared. They stank as well. She went past them, and nearing the open garage, saw the name 'Balsub' scrawled on the outside walls in dimmed charcoal letters. Next to the garage entrance, an iron grill closed off a large area. The door itself was curtained.

She called out softly, 'Sir' and heard a great growl in reply. When she peeped in carefully, she made out a cage from which an ape hung, staring at her. Its face was very close. It grinned, showing its teeth. Her heart beat fast. Immediately she drew back and called out loudly. Balsub came out. He looked very weak and tired. He joined the palms of his hands. 'Please come in,' he said.

'Were you scared at the sight of Maruti?' he asked. 'Didn't Gopi warn you?' He addressed himself to the ape, 'Maru, my pet, this is only our client. No one else.' Maruti sat down in a corner of his cage, staring blankly.

The front part of the garage had been partitioned off to make a reception room. The cage took up three-fourths of the space. A sofa had been placed right next to it.

'We could have sat here. But he hasn't been in a good mood for a couple of days. So let's go inside.'

Inside, a small space was set aside for the kitchen portion. A Marathi woman was cooking a meal there. There was a bed in the centre of the room. A sofa in one corner. A few chairs. A table. A keyboard, on top of the table. A tampura in another corner. A bookcase. A bureau. Beyond that, the bathroom, probably.

He sat down on the sofa, accepted the plastic folder she offered him, opened it and took out the pages. He set aside the Tamil manuscript, and began to read the English translation. After reading for a while he looked up and told her, 'I've totally forgotten how to read Tamil.'

He turned towards the woman who was cooking and said, 'Jijabai, *dhon cup chaha aan*. (Bring two cups of tea).'

'Where are you from?' he asked her after that.

'Chennai. George Town. Govindappa Naiker Street. What about yourself?'

'I'm from Chennai, too. Purasavakkam side.' He paused. Then, as if he was remembering these things after a very long time, he continued, 'My grandfather used to run a drama troupe there in those days. He was an actor of female roles. He had waist-length hair. When it was tied up, they say, it would sit on his head like a bronze pot. It seems women yearned to wear their saris in the way he wore his. He had a voice like the ringing of temple bells. He used to survey his audience keenly, it seems. If he saw anyone in the first three rows with an anxious expression, or looking as if they were disturbed at heart, that whole day he would sing the Sankarabaranam. Do you know this? If your mind is suffering from tension, or some kind of confusion, the Sankarabaranam will drain it all away. It will lighten the heart. If, at times, he saw one or two people with drooping eyes, he'd begin immediately, in the Bauli ragam, *Parvati nayaka . . .* "Parvati's consort . . ." As soon as he hit the high notes of the *anupallavi*, and sang the words, *Sarva lokaika natha . . .* "Lord of the entire universe . . ." their drowsiness would have vanished . . .'

Jijabai brought the tea and placed it on a small stool. Along with it, *aloo-poha* made with chopped potatoes, and the Maharashtrian version of beaten-rice *upma*.

'Help yourself,' he said.

Suddenly he said, 'Today is the fifteenth day since Mythili left us.'

'Who's Mythili?'

'My wife. This tampura is hers. She used to sing beautifully. Poor wretch, she'd melt you. Now she's gone . . .'

She tried to get up, hastily, saying, 'Forgive me sir; another day . . .' But he signalled to her to sit down.

'It was her time; she left us. What can we do? Her own son killed her . . .'

'Her son?'

'Yes. We think of Maruti as our own son. She used to fondle him and call him, "My Son, my Son".'

She could see the ape sitting in a corner of his cage, his cheek held in his hand.

'I once composed the music for the advertisements of a circus company. The owner of the circus became a close friend during that time. Since I went there frequently, this Maruti grew accustomed to me. He was a small fellow then. Eventually the owner gave him to me. When we reached home, he went up to Mythili directly and clung to her. Ever since then, he doted on her. Music was his very life. Whenever I played on the keyboard, he would listen intently. The instant Mythili started to tune her tampura, he'd begin to jump with joy. Immediately afterwards, he'd sit still and unmoving. He understands everything we say. Even now he can comprehend what we are talking about.'

He leaned across and looked at him. 'Maru, it's you I'm talking about. I'm telling her how Amma used to sing . . .' he said.

The ape made a sound like a sob, and covered its face.

'He feels sorry that he bit her . . .'

Shocked, she asked, 'Did he really bite her?'

'Yes. You know, he likes every ragam there is: Sahana, Kamaas, Desh . . . But you just could not sing Hamsadvani in his hearing. He'd go into a frenzy. Right from the beginning, he was like that. We had no idea why. I don't know if there was some resemblance between the music they played for his show in the circus, and Hamsadvani. Anyway, for his sake, Mythili left off singing Hamsadvani. It was Ganapathy Visarjan on that particular day. You know how it is. People go in great crowds, singing and chanting, to throw images of Ganapathi into the sea. Mythili and Maruti were alone in the house. Just two months ago, Mythili had had a heart attack. "If I am gone, then who is there for Maruti," she kept lamenting then. But when she heard all that rejoicing outside, as people thronged the streets, carrying the idols, she couldn't bear it any longer. "*Vinayaka . . .*" she began in Hamsadvani. Meltingly she sang, *Anatha rakshaga niive, kaadha . . .* "Are you not the saviour of the orphaned . . ." His cage wasn't locked, you see. He rushed out and gave her a single bite. She was in hospital for three days. She kept telling me, "Don't scold him!" Then she was gone . . .'

Balsub turned and looked at the cage. The ape was lying down now, all curled up. Balsub rose to his feet. 'Can you wait for me for fifteen minutes? I'll finish my bath and join you. Jijabai has to finish her work and leave. There are lots of books in the bookcase. Please read whatever you want. I'll be back soon.'

'Very well, sir.'

As soon as he left for his bath, Jijabai came to remove the plates and glasses from the stool. She asked in Marathi, 'Are you a Madrasi?'

'Yes,' she said.

'He only spoke the Madrasi language with Mythili Aayi. That's why he is talking so much today. He is on his own, poor man. He used to live in the big building in front, in a three-bedroom flat. For twenty years now, he's been living here. It was just music, music, music for the two of them. You should hear him sing Abhang. When Aayi sang, he'd accompany her on this wooden box. Crowds would gather at the threshold. They were happy in the three-bedroom flat. When they came to this garage, too, they came smiling. They never complained about anyone. The owners of the building themselves gave them special permission to stay here. Before this, Sahib's big car used to be garaged here.'

127

Jijabai sat down on the floor. Apparently, she too had no one to talk to.

'. . . It was I who forgot to bolt the door of the cage that day. When Maruti bit her, Aayi screamed out. It was evening time. There was a lot of noise outside. It was Visarjan that day. I had just left my bag and set off. I went as far as the gate, and then turned back. As I came near the rubbish bins, I could hear Aayi's voice. I came running inside. As I entered, Aayi said, "Jijabai, *Maruti malaa chaavala* . . . (Maruti has bitten me)". Maruti was standing next to the cage. I pushed him inside and drew the bolt. I telephoned their daughter, but she never came. The chowkidar and I had to take her to the hospital ourselves. Just three days. Aayi was gone . . .'

Balsub came out of the bathroom. 'Well, has Jijabai finished telling her story?' Jijabai smiled, and went away to wash the clothes.

He sat down again on the sofa. 'You've come a long distance,' he said. 'I'll certainly read your story. If I can't do it myself, I have many disciples. One of them will do the music for you. Don't worry.'

'May I say goodbye then?'

'Yes, do that. I have to lie down for a little while. This is a small house. I am not able to ask you to stay here a little longer. But please rest on the sofa outside, if you like, until the heat dies down somewhat.'

She didn't think she could spend any more time gazing at the ape who hated Hamsadvani. It would be far better to take the train to Mira Road. She said goodbye, came out and had just set off towards the gate, when a woman of forty to forty-five approached her. 'Who did you come to visit?' the woman asked in English.

'Balsub . . .'

'And have you taken a look at the ape?'

'Do you mean Maruti?'

'That's the ape in the cage. I meant the ape outside the cage.'

'Balsub . . .'

'That's the ape. Has it gone to sleep?'

'And you are?'

'I'm his daughter. I'm the one in the flat in the front building.'

'I'm just leaving.'

'Jijabai must have complained to you that I didn't turn up when Amma called out.'

'She told me.'

'And why should I come? That ape was more important to them than I. They even wanted that murderous animal to do the last rites for her. Have you ever heard of such a thing?' Her voice shook. 'Appa and Amma taught me music from the time I was five years old. All right, so this ape turned up here. But it was my music that came to harm because of his arrival. Do you know, Madam, a *kiirtanai* in Hamsadvani ragam was my first *kiirtanai*. And a *varnam* in Hamsadvani was my very first *varnam*. I struggled for fifteen years because I couldn't sing that ragam in our house. If I even hummed it the ape would start leaping in fury. It was after that, I sent them away to the garage. Have you seen the place? Can it be called a home? Yet they lived there very happily, for twenty years, with their ape. I am free to sing Hamsadvani now, Madam. I can sing it as loudly as I wish. But I can't. In my mind's eye I see the ape leaping in his cage. My tongue falters.'

She was breathing hard.

'Look, I'm on my way there, even now. To visit the ape who lives in the cage as well as the ape outside it.' She spat out the words.

All through the long train journey to Mira Road, her mind was choked up by the thought of a big cage and an ape which leapt with fury when it heard Hamsadvani.

In the end, it was one of the disciples who composed the music for her film. He avoided Hamsadvani. He composed it in Malayamarutam. His pet cat's favourite ragam, apparently.

Journey 9

There were no trains departing from Churchgate to Andheri that day. She had to go to V.T. and take the local train to Chembur. This was a journey that had come about quite suddenly. Amma was not well, and had asked to see her. Her elder brother had ordered her to go to his home directly from her office. She could not refuse. In earlier days, her mother would speak to her on the telephone, at great length. There was no one else with whom she could discuss Tamil Nadu politics. She would watch the TV serials in Tamil, without fail, besides. She was keen on literature too. She'd complain that Vannanilavan had not written anything for a long time. When she grew hard of hearing, she could no longer hold long telephone conversations. Her brother's family had lost their interest in Tamil Nadu and the Tamil language. Whatever contact they might have had with these matters, through Amma, had worn threadbare. That's why her mother was seized by a sudden longing to talk to her from time to time. She'd make herself ill because of it. As soon as she went there and talked with her a little, Amma would feel much better. She made this journey to her brother's house at the weekends usually. This was the first time she was doing it mid-week.

She took the bus to V.T., got off at the station, and set off amidst the press of the crowds, towards her platform, suddenly overcome with tiredness. The burden of work from her office sat heavily upon her shoulders like some kind of demon. During the last month they had two resignations. A complaint about the behaviour of a coordinator. Two applications for maternity leave. The office was crippled, unable to run properly.

There was a long queue at the ticket office. She joined the queue, bought her ticket, and looked up at the announcement board hanging above. Her train had not been announced yet. Three ceiling fans were suspended, just next to the announcement board. If she stood there, she wouldn't stream with sweat. She could also keep a close watch on the announcements. There were a few others standing there, reading a newspaper or a book. She joined them and wiped her face with a handkerchief. She stood there, keeping an eye on the board and gazing at the people coming and going, at the same time.

Crowds of people were streaming in and out of both the entrance and the exit to the station. Seen through narrowed eyes, it was almost as if there was a vessel with two spouts from which a multi-coloured mixture was pouring out.

This railway wasn't like the western line. This one served Mumbai's long central area, as well as a wide section which ran parallel to the harbour. People who travelled along this line had different needs and lifestyles. Because the main line station serving the lines that went out of

Mumbai was right next to this one, the luggage carried by the passengers was different in shape and weight as well. As she watched, suitcases on wheels and tin trunks, babies packaged in fine clothes and naked babies, hats, colourful turbans, cloth bundles, expensive shoes and bare feet all raced past her eyes like hastily drawn lines.

Suddenly, coming from somewhere to her side, an arm loomed in front. The palm of the hand held a small white card; the reverse side of a calling card with a name and address. It said in English, in distinct black letters 'Only Rs 100 per service. 100% satisfaction guaranteed.'

For a moment she didn't understand what service was meant, and what satisfaction. When she realized what it was, she was extremely startled. She looked through the corner of her eyes at the individual who had extended the card towards her, and then withdrawn it in a second. A young man. Twenty-five years old, or thereabouts. A man who believed he could guarantee 100 per cent satisfaction. Did she look like a woman who was searching for 100 per cent satisfaction? What would such a woman look like, anyway?

Slowly she turned round and looked at him. He was staring ahead as if he were totally innocent.

She spoke to him in Hindi, 'Excuse me, what's your name, please?'

'Why Madam?' he asked, covered in confusion.

'For no reason. Shouldn't I know the name of someone who is offering me his services?'

'Please forgive me, Madam. If I've done something wrong . . .'

'Don't worry. I just asked.'

'Gopal Misra,' he muttered.

'From U.P.?'

He nodded. He looked haggard; extremely weary.

'Shall we have some tea, Misraji?'

He brightened up at once. It was obvious he thought he had found a customer. They went to a tea stall right inside the station. She bought him a sandwich and a packet of *bonda*s. He took them from her, and ate hungrily. She bought two paper cups of tea and handed him one. '*Dhanyavad*, thank you,' he muttered, accepting it and drinking. He would not look up at her.

'I think, Misraji, you haven't eaten anything since this morning.'

'That's true, Madam.'

'What do you do, for your livelihood?'

He was silent.

'So is this all you do? This service which gives 100 per cent satisfaction?'

'Yes,' he said in a low voice, his head bowed.

'So how much do you make in a day?'

'Some days I get over a thousand. On other days, there will be no work at all.'

'Is the Central–Harbour line where you work?'

He nodded.

It seemed that all the women who lacked satisfaction travelled on this line alone.

'Why did you choose this line?'

'There are many conveniences to this place, Madam. It's easy to get rooms nearby. Sometimes you can get well-appointed houses, too.'

'Misraji, how do you select your customers?'

'That is . . . It's a sort of guess . . .'

'So what do unsatisfied women look like?'

'They tend to be restless. They shift from one leg to the other. Their eyes keep wandering. They look thoughtful. They are usually in their thirties or forties.'

'Do you never make a mistake in your supposition?'

'Ninety-nine per cent of the time there isn't a mistake, Madam.'

Appa! Were there so many women on the lookout for people like Misra?

'So did I look like that too?'

'Arré, Madam . . .' he writhed with embarrassment. 'Madam, you looked very tense. You kept wiping your face. You kept on looking around you . . . so . . .'

'Misraji, I'm on my way to see my mother. I've come here directly from my office. I have to go to Chembur, and then on to Andheri. I have to get home and cook an evening meal. Besides, there's all this crowd, isn't there? That's why I was a little tense. Otherwise, I am not in need of 100 per cent satisfaction at the moment, I think . . .'

'Madam, in that case . . .'

His frustration at having wasted time with someone who did not wish to be a client was apparent.

She opened her bag and took out a hundred-rupee note.

'I have taken up your working time, haven't I? Take this. But some day you must tell me about this 100 per cent satisfaction. I'm very interested to know how that could be.'

He took the hundred-rupee note from her. 'Madam, you've given me this. I can give you all the details right now. What women really desire . . .'

'Excuse me, Misraji. I have no time now. The Chembur train is about to arrive. If we ever meet again some day . . .' saying this, she hurried away.

135

She only realized that along with the hundred rupees, she had lost one of her cards with her address and details, when he telephoned her one night, at about one o'clock.

It was six months later, one night, when the telephone rang. It rang without stopping. She picked it up and heard Gopal Misra's voice.

'Madam, I'm Gopal Misra . . .' His voice sounded broken, as if he were close to tears.

She had forgotten him completely. 'What Gopal Misra? Sorry, wrong number . . .'

'Madam, Madam,' he shouted. 'Please Madam, don't put the phone down. I'm Gopal Misra. We met at V.T. station when you were on your way to Chembur, and talked.'

She remembered him then.

'Madam, please . . . May I come up to your flat? I feel as if I'm about to faint, Madam . . .'

'Wait by the gate. I'll come down,' she told him, putting the receiver down.

In Mumbai, you had to be careful of inviting even acquaintances to your flat at one o'clock at night, when you were on your own. She had a few things ready, for self-defence. A spray of black pepper, for one. Sprinkled on the eyes, it would make them burn, cause the head to spin. The other weapon was an ancient one, a wedding gift to her mother from her parents. When she was a young girl, Amma had used it to pound chillies, and the flour for *appalam*. When Amma moved to Mumbai, this was one of the objects rejected by everyone as useless, but donated to her all the same by her mother. Amma hated to abandon anything. It was a heavy, long-handled wooden pestle with an iron collar. She kept it hidden behind a door. She had decided that any house-breaker would be dealt a single blow with it.

She locked her front door and went downstairs. She told the watchman at the gate, 'Watchman, I'm expecting a friend who isn't well. Please help me find him a taxi.'

In about ten minutes Gopal Misra walked slowly towards them, searching for the right building. He looked extremely distressed. He staggered as he walked. His whole body was shuddering. His face was swollen, his lip torn at one end. When he saw her, he began to sob, 'Madam . . .'

'Misraji, if I put you into a taxi, will you be able to go home?'

When she said this, he started to cry, saying, 'Madam, I'll lie down here in the garden, if you prefer. I simply haven't the strength in my body, Madam.'

She asked the watchman to bring him upstairs. He signed the visitors' register with trembling hands. Meanwhile, she hastened upstairs, to open the front door.

He came up, the watchman holding him and helping him along. She asked him to sit down on the sofa in the hall.

She caught him as he was about to fall down, and made him sit on her sofa. 'Misraji, there's a geyser in the bathroom. Go and wash your face, arms and legs in hot water,' she said, sympathetically.

His eyes filled with tears. He struggled to his feet and staggered off towards the bathroom.

She filled a vessel with water for tea, and placed it on the stove. She sliced in some ginger. The tea was ready by the time he returned. She filled a plate with the upma left over from her evening meal, and placed it and the tea on a small stool beside the sofa. She brought a tumbler of water.

'Help yourself,' she said.

He struggled to swallow a mouthful of water. His lip must have been burning. She handed him some coconut oil, and told him to apply that.

Gradually he began to eat. He didn't speak. When he started on his tea, she asked, 'What happened, Misraji? Was there a fight? Did someone attack you?' If he could recover himself a little, she would put him in a taxi, with the watchman's help, she thought.

He began to cry again. He was in tears as he drank his tea. In the middle of sobs, he said, 'There was no fight, Madam.'

He finished his tea. 'I'm sorry, Madam. I've put you to a lot of trouble. Your card fell out along with the hundred-rupee note that day . . .' he said. Then, 'Madam, at about seven o'clock, I was able to fix up a very good customer. About forty-five years old. She said to me, "There are a couple more of us. Will you come to my house? I'll give you five hundred rupees." I agreed. She must have come to the station on some other business. She had a car. We came to Andheri in it.'

It didn't look as if she would be able to send him away quickly. 'Where in Andheri?' she asked.

He gave her the address to which the woman had taken him.

It was quite near her home, that address. It appeared that the women seeking Misraji's service were located in all parts of Mumbai. There were many thousands of houses. How many secrets, in the course of day-to-day living, were hidden within them?

Gopal Misra leaned against the sofa and continued to mutter. 'At first it was all right, Madam. But gradually it all turned frightful. They tied me up in chains; struck at me with a belt; bit me; slashed me with a razor blade; made me go on all fours like a dog . . . They tortured me, madam.'

He opened his shirt to show her. There were red welts all over his body, where he was beaten with the belt. The slashes were still bleeding, besides. It was difficult to make out where he had been bitten. It became clear to her that he was in no state to go home yet. She could see no solution, other than letting him stay overnight.

She rose to her feet and brought him a bottle of Dettol and some cotton wool. She fetched some Calendula ointment. 'Be very careful hereafter, Misraji,' she told him. 'It isn't right to trouble people in this way, and at this time of night.'

His eyes filled. He went into the bathroom and applied medicine all over himself. Both the Dettol and the ointment were completely used up. Could he be so badly hurt?

She pulled out the settee to make a convenient bed. His hand was burning hot as he stretched it out to take the sheet from her. Burning with fever.

He lay down and covered himself with the sheet. He continued to talk as he lay there.

'After doing all that, they drove me out forcibly, saying I hadn't give them 100 per cent satisfaction, madam. They didn't give me the agreed fee. They even grabbed what little I had. There was just a rupee coin and that card you gave me long ago, left in my purse, madam.' Sunk in self-pity, he started to cry all over again.

She gave him a Crocin tablet and told him to swallow it with plenty of water.

Still he lamented, calling out as if in a delirium, 'Ei Gauri. Ei Gauri . . .'

'Who is Gauri?'

'My wife. She lives in the village . . .'

At last, still weeping, he fell asleep. All through the night, his confused ramblings reached her bedside, within the flat.

In the morning she gave him a cup of tea, and an old shirt out of the store of clothes her friend Raghuvir kept in her flat, and wore when he visited her from Delhi, from time to time. Brokenly, his throat choking, he said he didn't know how to thank her.

The fever had abated. When she gave him money for a taxi, the tears began to flow again.

'What is this, Misraji, should you weep like this?'

'They complained that they didn't get 100 per cent satisfaction, madam. My service has been disgraced . . .' he said.

'No one can guess what is 100 per cent and for whom. You ask Gauri, she'll tell you.'

As soon as she mentioned Gauri, his features brightened up. He wiped away his tears and smiled. It was clear that as far as Gauri was concerned, there were no doubts in his mind.

There was no knowing whether after that the guarantees he offered changed, or whether, indeed, his entire means of livelihood changed. She never saw Gopal Misra again.

Journey 10

Emily had come to the airport to meet her, as promised. The city she encountered as they came out of the airport looked like a *rakshasa* who had been destroyed. A demon who had fallen, caught unaware by an arrow entering his back. A rakshasa who had gone his own way, not pestering anyone.

A city in a totally dilapidated state. Derelict buildings everywhere. Imphal looked as if destroyed by a war, and in ruins, as yet unrestored. The hotel was located in a narrow, crowded road, known as the main street. An Indian military jeep stood at the entrance. Inside it, there were two soldiers bearing guns, looking as if they were ready to make war at any moment. Cycle rickshaws were driven here and there by men who had covered their faces entirely.

Emily was in a hurry to leave, as soon as she had made all the appropriate arrangements at the hotel. It was difficult to understand why she was in such a rush. It was still only four thirty in the afternoon. She finished her hastily ordered tea in two or three gulps, and fled.

Within fifteen minutes of her departure, it began to darken. By half past five, it was completely dark. The street down below was silent. Her hotel room was tiny, with two small windows. One of them was shut tightly; she had been told by the hotel's employee not to open it. She could see the silent street through the other window.

The chirping of birds sounded very close to her, tearing through the darkness. The two soldiers sitting in the jeep looked up towards her window.

She moved away from the window and sat down on her bed. Did that girl from Manipur, caught up among the crowds of Mumbai, experience this same feeling that was overwhelming her now? The very day before the incident, she had said, 'Nobody considers us as Indians.'

A week before that, the festival she had arranged exhibiting handicrafts, paintings and films from the North-eastern states had failed miserably. Someone had even asked, 'Where's Mizoram?' When he was informed that it was one of the states of India, he replied that she clearly didn't know any geography. Another person asked, 'How can people with slit eyes and flat noses be Indians?'

The electricity failed during a Manipuri dance performance, but their stage managers had not been bothered in the least. The dancers had performed to candlelight, without worrying. When she apologized, they merely said, 'But there were the candles, weren't there? We have danced even by moonlight. We can do it.'

There had been only five in the audience every day, when the films from the North-east were shown. Not a single individual showed up to interview the artists who had come from there. One of the spectators had contacted her by email, later. She was a fool, he suggested, ignorant of cinema; why else would she bring these flat-nosed people to a city such as Mumbai, famous for its celebrities like Amitabh Bachchan and Shahrukh Khan? He was prepared to give her a lesson or two, provided, that is, she could pay him a fee.

It was a little after this that the incident happened. Because the two events happened one after the other, they were linked in her mind. Out of all the people, dwellers of Mumbai as well as tourists, crowded by the Gateway of India, gazing with enjoyment at the sea, a madman targetted a girl from Manipur, and killed her. She gave up her life, calling out, 'Don't kill me, I'm an Indian citizen; I'm an Indian citizen.'

And now here she was, on a preview tour. A journey she was undertaking on behalf of a voluntary organization, to find out what sort of projects might be workable in the North-eastern states.

When she looked out of the window again, she could see the gun, held aloft by the soldier, glowing in the moonlight.

In the morning, Emily arrived in an ancient car. Her younger brother was to drive them around.

She suggested that they have some fruit for their breakfast. It was only when she asked the price of the fruit that she realized it would be a five-star breakfast. The car set off towards a village, three hours away. There was an orphanage there, set up to look after the children who were orphaned by the fights between the Kuki and Naga tribes. A woman and her husband ran the institution. One of the objectives of her journey was to meet this woman and discuss things with her.

On both sides of the road, as they travelled by car, mountains covered in green rose high. A green that stroked the eyes. The blue of the skies scattered everywhere. Clouds, rich as butter. Eating her apple with relish, Emily warned, 'Madam, very soon we'll be arriving at an army checkpoint. Don't be scared. Just be natural. Nothing will happen.'

She had a camera and a tape recorder with her. She told herself that Emily should have warned her earlier about the checkpoint.

At a little distance, a bus had been stopped and made to park to one side. The travellers stood at both sides of the road, gazing at the green mountains, their hands held at their backs. The soldiers were questioning them and prodding at their luggage.

Their car was stopped. Two soldiers came up, one on either side of the vehicle. One of them spoke to Emily, who answered them in the same language. She could hear the name of the village they were bound for, mentioned. Emily pointed to her and said something about Mumbai. When she finished speaking, the soldier moved round and gazed steadily at her through the car window, for half a second. A face of stone. Eyes drained of light. She had never seen a soldier so close. She had a friend who was a major in the army. Every morning, an orderly came to help him get ready, by polishing his brass buttons. 'Your face tightens up as soon as you get into your uniform,' she used to tease him. 'It's all your imagination,' he'd reply, immediately bursting into Rabindra Sangeet. Or else, he'd sing, in Pankaj Malik's voice, '*Tere mandir ka hun dipak*; I am a lamp in your temple'

'There's absolutely no connection between your uniform and your song, Bengali Babu,' she would say. He'd laugh loudly, then.

It didn't look as if this staring soldier was likely to sing at any stage of his life. A face that was utterly dead. Metallic eyes. Her spine grew cold.

He waved the car on. It started again.

'What did he ask, Emily?'

'The usual questions, madam. What's your business at the orphanage, why you have come from Mumbai, and so on.'

'So what did you say?'

'You have a soft heart, I said. You heard about this place through a friend. You don't have any children of your own. That's a great sorrow in your life. That's one reason for coming so far.'

'You tell a good story.'

'Do you have children?'

'No.'

'Do you like them, or not?'

'Of course I do.'

'Then what's wrong with what I said?'

'You take some facts which are true and twist them to suit yourself.'

Emily laughed.

There were several more army checkpoints after that. Emily added many more pitiful details to her story, all of them spoken in a steady and unwavering voice. The lady's womb had been removed when she was still young. She had suffered a kind of mental illness for five years, because of her childlessness. She was only just recovering from that. Whenever she heard of an orphanage, she set off towards it. Weren't these enough reasons for her to travel this far?

The harsh look didn't disappear from the soldiers' faces. But they gave their permission and moved them on.

She was in danger of believing Emily's story herself, by the time they neared the orphanage.

They arrived. The children ranged from four- to fifteen-year-olds. They lived in small, hermitage-like houses made of woven bamboo; fifteen to twenty in each. There were bunk beds, stacked one above the other. All around them were mountains, filling their eyes. A small chapel with a single wooden cross. She spoke to the director of the ashram, recording their conversation.

'We only have children here who are completely orphaned. We give them an education here. We hope to send them on to college, later . . .

'They only have two meals a day. One at 8.30 in the morning, the other at 4.30 in the afternoon . . .

'We don't get any milk here. These children have never drunk any milk. There is no milk in any of the houses here. They enjoy fruits only if and when anybody donates some . . .'

During the conversation, a little girl who she had noticed before, brought her a cup of tea without milk, and placed it next to her along with a couple of biscuits.

'How long has this little girl been here?'

'She is eight years old. She's my daughter.'

'I saw her in one of the children's houses. That's why . . .'

'I have two children. They grow up with all the others. I have a very large family. All these children call my husband Daddy. They call me Mummy.'

Gradually the children, all of them, gathered near. They gazed at her as if she were some kind of wonder.

She called them to her, and they came and sat around, in a circle. She said to the director, 'Ask them to tell me what they want.'

Their faces brightened. Gesticulating enthusiastically, they began to explain. One child would agree with another, the older children expanding vociferously on what was said. Eyes widened, heads nodded, hands were spread wide and held apart . . .

The director interpreted for her. 'They say they want a big library. They want lots and lots of books, with stories printed on glossy paper and pictures in bright colours. Stories about kings and queens, adventure stories, world famous stories, they want them all. They want wooden bookcases full of books, they say. They suggest that the chapel is converted into a library.'

'We can get lots of CDs with children's songs, pictures and stories. Wouldn't they like those?'

'No. You see they all have to sit together to view those CDs. They prefer to find their own corner and hold a book in their own hands. They say they like the feel of paper. They want to touch and stroke the coloured pictures. That's what they were telling you, at such length.'

She looked at the children and asked, 'Really?'

'Yes, Aunty,' they chorused.

These were children of the hills. They needed the warmth of the body. They didn't relish anything which they couldn't touch with their hands, with the dirt and sweat of their hands. Electricity had indeed entered their world. When she was shown around the ashram, she had seen a few computers. Yet they needed the sensation of touch. They stood, smeared in earth, even in this world of electronic power.

Emily drove the car on their return. She said she had obtained her licence only a month ago. Her body ached all over, when the soldiers' questioning and Emily's adventurous driving came to an end, at last.

They parked the car at the hotel entrance, and went to the Ima market. This was a daily market run by women. The women from the surrounding villages had brought handloom materials, clothes, jewellery, objects crafted from metal or wood, vegetables, eggs and sold them there; or ran food stalls, preparing and serving food on the premises. The market was just about to close, otherwise they could have eaten there, Emily said. They went past the market to a little lane behind it. Emily led her to a small restaurant. 'This is a place where workers come to eat. The food is very good, and it's cheap as well.' she said.

The plates came, full of rotis, dal, and a potato preparation. The potato dish was full of small nuts, the size of a pea. Emily cracked them between her teeth and ate them. All around there was the snapping sound of nuts being split open. Obviously you needed special teeth to deal with the nuts. Quietly she set them to one side. There was another vegetable too.

'What's this?'

'Oh, that's lotus stem.'

She had seen them in the Ima market. Some people were selling lotus blossoms too.

By the time they returned to the hotel, it was past five. Emily said goodbye, and left in a hurry.

It grew dark.

She couldn't breathe in her room. Suddenly she heard the high-pitched chirping of birds. She looked at the tightly closed window. She would be leaving the next morning. What would happen if she were to open the window now?

She flung it open. Immediately, she called out, startled. Just outside, tiny black birds clustered, like bees surrounding a hive. As soon as she opened the window, hundreds of them flew inside, circling around and screeching excitedly. Their noise was comforting to her; companionable. She didn't know the names of these tiny birds. She'd have to check in Salim Ali's book. Or if she were to ask Theodore Baskaran, he would give her a beautiful Tamil name for them. But these were not singers in a grove. They were city singers. Night-time singers in a ruined city with an army camp. Birds which had not forgotten their song.

There were still these black birds here. If lotus stem curry was being cooked and served, then there must be ponds too, somewhere, where the lotus floated, still. At a distance, in a hill village, there were children who wanted books to read, with pages they could touch.

The birds circled her room for five minutes, and then flew away through her window.

When she looked out of the window, she saw one of the birds, more zealous than the rest, swoop down as if it were diving into a swimming pool, and settle on the tip of the gun, held upright by the soldier sitting in the jeep below. It sat there and flapped its tail up and down agitatedly, calling out in its shrillest voice.